*A
Harlequin
Romance*

Harlequin Romances
by LUCY GILLEN

GLEN OF SIGHS

by

LUCY GILLEN

HARLEQUIN BOOKS   TORONTO
WINNIPEG

Original hard cover edition published in 1972
by Mills & Boon Limited.

© Lucy Gillen 1972

SBN 373-01895-9

Harlequin edition published July 1975

Printed in Canada

CHAPTER ONE

THE train was late and Nicola felt tired and hungry as she stepped down on to the short, windy stretch of concrete that was the platform at Malin station. At least she assumed that there was no mistake on the worn wooden name board that sat atop a row of equally worn railings. The stark bareness of it was discouraging and she would have felt a little more encouraged if the one and only other human being in sight had not waved the train off and then walked off as if she did not exist.

She had expected Curran to send someone to meet her, perhaps even accompany whoever it was. He could not drive himself, she knew that well enough, because he had injured a leg in a riding accident only a week ago, but this deserted, unwelcoming station with no one at all to greet her was quite unexpected and very discouraging.

She followed the ticket collector-cum-porter in to the tiny brick hut that served as Malin station, and the man turned round to look at her curiously. Nicola put down her suitcases and looked at him, hopefully, putting on her nicest smile, just in case it would help. It usually did, for she was a very attractive girl.

'I'm sorry,' she said, unsure just why she was apologizing 'Are you in charge here?'

'I am, miss.' The man's dour face brightened a little as he took better stock of her, and he looked a bit less resentful, she thought.

'I was expecting someone to meet me from Malinbrae,' she explained. 'I don't seem to see anyone here. Could I have missed them, do you think?'

He shook his head with certainty. 'No, there's been no one here from Malinbrae today, miss,' he assured her, but the narrow blue eyes, she thought, looked even more interested at the mention of her destination and he regarded her for a moment. 'Ye'll be the young lady they're expectin',' he guessed, and Nicola nodded hopefully. Perhaps there was a message for her at least.

She had started out so very early that morning and the journey, while intensely interesting, had been long and tiring. She had breakfasted but not bothered about lunching on the train because she had been too interested in the changing scene as the train sped northwards and over the border. Too excited, too, at the prospect before her. Now it was getting quite late in the day and her stomach was protesting about its lack of nourishment, and her head was beginning to ache rather.

She had visualized being met at Malin station and quickly whisked off to Malinbrae and a very welcome dinner; instead here she was apparently abandoned on a bare little station and no sign of anyone to meet her. She had no idea how far it was to the house, even. Surely Curran could not have forgotten that it was today she arrived?

Even the idea of that made her smile, for Curran McCrae was just about as ardent a suitor as any girl ever had, and his success in getting her to join him at Malinbrae and meet his family had been the crowning achievement of months of persuasion.

Originally he was to have come down to the Midlands and fetched her, but that fall from a horse had precluded any idea of that, and she had agreed to travel up by train.

She smiled at the man again and he thawed visibly, his eyes appreciative of the picture she made, despite the effects of the journey. Wide-set grey eyes looked almost childishly appealing and the small oval face was beautiful by anyone's standards. The thick, bronzy-coloured hair that framed it was cut into a heavy half fringe that covered half the smooth brow and curled up at the ends just level with her jaw.

The smile was irresistible, and the man responded to it as many had done before, pushing his cap to the back of his head, and exploring the short grey thatch beneath it. 'Mebbe they left it a wee bit late settin' out,' he guessed. 'An' ye cannae hurry wi' the state o' that road.'

It was scarcely encouraging news, but at least it explained her apparent desertion and cheered her a little even if her stomach was still crying out for satisfaction.

'That road's in a shockin' state,' her informant went on, apparently grinding some personal axe, 'an' gettin'

7

worse every year.'

Nicola, uninterested in the shortcomings of the local council or whatever the Scottish equivalent was, looked along the narrow, stony road she could see from the platform, and frowned. There was still no sign of anyone coming, and she had not the least desire to tackle the allegedly bad road on foot and carrying two suitcases. Surely, she thought, there must be a taxi or a hire car, even out here.

'Perhaps I'd better find my own way there,' she suggested not very enthusiastically.

The station staff looked at her for a moment, speculatively, pulling at his lower lip. 'Ye could start ta walk,' he told her. 'There's no other way, I'm afraid. It's no so very far for a young creature like ye'sel',' he added when she looked at him in dismay, 'an' ye'll likely meet ye're party on the way.'

Nicola sighed. 'I don't mind walking normally, but I don't relish carrying my suitcases as well. I suppose there isn't a taxi?' she ventured hopefully.

'Aye, there is,' he replied, 'but he's away out ta Strathgorm w' old Mr. McDonald, an' he'll no be back for another hour mebbe.'

'Oh, I see.' Nicola sighed resignedly. 'Is there a telephone I could use?'

'Aye, there is, if ye'd come away in ta the office here.' He led the way into the inner sanctum of the brick hut and showed her an ancient instrument of the candlestick variety. 'It's no a very guid line,' he informed her, 'but ye're welcome to use it. Have ye the

8

number?'

She said she had, and dialled it on the ancient telephone while he left her in sole possession. He was quite right, she discovered after a moment or two, it *was* a bad line, but eventually a disembodied voice announced that she was connected with Malinbrae.

Someone, she was informed, it sounded rather like Migant, was on his way to meet her, and she gathered he should be there at any minute. She thanked her informant and rejoined the man on the platform, who looked at her inquiringly.

'I think I'll just wait outside by the road,' she informed him. 'Someone's on the way to pick me up.'

He gave her a hand with her cases and she stood outside on the stony road, hopefully. Seen from here the road was in an even worse condition than she had expected, scarred with numerous holes and bumps, and she shuddered to think what walking along it with two heavy suitcases would have resulted in.

She had stood there for nearly ten minutes before there was any sign of anyone coming. Sound carried remarkably in this quiet, open country and she lifted her head when she caught the sound of a car approaching, some distance off as yet, she suspected. It would almost certainly be her tardy reception committee, and she prepared a frown of disapproval for his arrival.

The sound of the approaching car grew louder and she blinked in surprise a moment later when at last it came into view. It was huge, shiny and American, and it came round the first corner at a speed that startled her, and at the same time gave her a sudden feeling of disappointment.

It was doubtful if this was the car she had been waiting for. It was far more likely to be some wealthy American tourist visiting the Highlands than her expected escort, judging by the size and opulence of the vehicle. Curran always drove a quiet, respectable English car and she could not imagine him or any of his family owning such a showy monster as this.

Surprisingly, however, it braked to a halt beside her and the driver got out, smiling at her curiously. 'Hi!' He raised one hand in greeting, confirming his nationality. 'I guess I'm late.'

'Late?' For a moment she forgot that he had kept her waiting, she was too surprised by his appearance.

'You *are* Nicola Scott, aren't you?' he asked, and she frowned anew at the easy way he used both her names. Surely Miss Scott would have been more in keeping from a stranger who was probably only a member of the staff at Malinbrae. She nodded, however, without saying a word and he picked up her cases from the road. 'Then it's you I'm supposed to meet,' he said.

'You *are* late,' she told him shortly. 'I've been waiting here for some time.'

He paused in the act of putting her suitcases into the back of the car, and elevated one brow as if her reaction was not what he expected, but he was not perturbed by it, that much was obvious. 'Well now, I'm sure sorry about that, honey,' he drawled. 'But I guess those doggone potholes held me up some.'

She felt sure his accent had not been as pronounced as that initially, and she frowned her dislike of the familiar 'honey'. It was an Americanism she detested. 'I know all about the road,' she told him, 'but surely you could have started out early enough to give yourself time.'

He laughed, and she hastily lowered her eyes, because he was looking at her in such a way she could feel her heart banging away nervously against her ribs and it made her feel suddenly wary and uneasy. She was not at all sure that she felt like trusting herself to this impudent and disconcerting stranger, no matter if Curran had sent him.

'You come right out with it, don't you?' he asked, and laughed again. 'Come on, get in and I'll deliver you to your lord and master.'

'Who are you?' she demanded, gasping at this new insolence, and making no move as yet to accept the invitation of the door he held open for her.

He regarded her for a moment, half serious, and still amused. 'You mean you don't trust me?'

The suggestion seemed to amuse him further and Nicola knew her cheeks were flaming as she carefully avoided looking at him. 'I – I mean I've never heard Curran – Mr. McCrae mention anyone like you,' she told him.

'I guess you wouldn't,' he allowed. 'I'm not Curran's favourite cousin and he prefers not to remember whenever possible.' He stood beside the huge opulence of the car, watching her and wearing a smile that she found even more unnerving. 'I'm Mitchell Grant the second, Mitch to my friends,' he announced. 'Now, will you get in the car and let's get started?'

'Oh, I see.' She thought, searching her memory, that she remembered Curran at some time mentioning that he had an uncle in America, so maybe this man was his son, since he claimed kinship.

He smiled again, a curiously slow smile that crooked his mouth at one corner. 'Good – now if you're satisfied with my credentials perhaps we could go.'

He slammed the door after her and came round and tucked his long legs under the steering wheel, chuckling softly when she instinctively hunched away from him. The road was if anything a little worse as they drove along and she could understand his reluctance to hurry on the outward journey, breathing a sigh of relief when at last they turned in to a tree-lined drive.

It was much more even and surfaced with gravel, and she looked along it curiously at the house at the far end. Malinbrae was built on a slight hill, and sat amid its guardian trees looking quiet and peaceful, just as Curran had always said it did, mellow in the warm August sun that caught the panes in the high windows and blinked back at her.

Two huge oak doors guarded the front entrance and looked very imposing so that she felt a qualm of worry over her own possible welcome. There was no doubt at all that Curran would be glad to see her again, but she had never met the rest of his family, his father and an aunt, and she was very uncertain how they would receive someone from a very different background from themselves.

The McCraes, so Curran had told her, were a very old family and had lived in this part of the Highlands for centuries, so that pride of family was bound to be part of their heritage. How they would take to an ordinary middle-class girl like herself, she was in some doubt, despite Curran's assurances that they would love her as he did.

Curran's mother was dead, and had been for some years now, and Curran was an only child. He had been schooled in England and trained to be an engineer, although he had now forsaken it for the quiet, more traditional role of manager of the vast estate which would one day be his.

Nicola had been a typist on the staff of the company he was with when they met, and he had lost no time in singling her out for his special attention. Then, when he left to return to Scotland, they had corresponded fairly frequently and he had even been down to see her a couple of times.

At last he had managed to persuade her to come up to Scotland and meet his family, only to take a fall from his horse which prevented him from fetching her. It would have been less of an ordeal to have travelled up with Curran.

She blinked herself out of her reverie when her escort opened the car door and waited for her to get out.

'O.K.?' he inquired, hefting her suitcases from the back seat, and Nicola nodded silently, her whole attention on the big rambling old house.

He led the way up a couple of shallow, worn steps to the impressive oak doors, using a shoulder to push one of them open. 'Here we are.' He put down her cases and stood looking at her. 'I guess Curran's around somewhere,' he said. 'I'll give him a yell.'

It was unnecessary, however, for the door behind him opened almost at once and Curran McCrae hobbled out, using a stick to help him to walk. He came forward eagerly, one arm outstretched to hug her close, his brown eyes bright with the pleasure of seeing her again. 'Nicola!' His arms closed round her. 'Oh, it's so good to see you again! Welcome to Malinbrae.'

He was tall and quite heavily built for a man of his age and his face still had a round boyishness about it, but he was good-looking and quite definitely attractive and, Nicola often suspected, not as naïve as he looked. He held her away from him for a moment, studying her, as if he could never see enough of her. 'Did you have a good journey, darling?'

'Very good,' Nicola smiled, 'but very long and rather dirty, and I skipped lunch because I was so busy looking at the scenery.'

'No lunch?' He looked horrified. 'Oh, my poor sweet, you must be starving!'

'I am,' she admitted ruefully, and he hugged her again, seeming to notice his cousin for the first time, standing beside her suitcases. 'Thanks for fetching her for me, Mitchell.'

Mitchell, she noticed, not Mitch, as he claimed his friends called him. Apparently Curran was not very enthusiastic about him, as he had said. 'Any time.' He smiled at Nicola, and she really saw him for the first time.

He was perhaps thirty-five or six years old, quite a bit older than Curran, and well over six feet tall, dwarfing her own rather petite stature. Dark brown hair, not quite black, flopped untidily over one eye and he ran his fingers through it carelessly, unperturbed, even amused, by her scrutiny.

He had a rangy slimness that somehow suggested quickness and strength, an impression added to by long, lean legs in close-fitting blue jeans. His face too matched the rest of him, strong-looking and with high cheekbones slimming down to a square, stubborn-looking chin, and blue eyes whose upper lids were fringed with quite long lashes for a man.

And, she recognized with a flicker of quickening pulse, there was no mistaking that Mitchell Grant was a man, for he flaunted his masculinity like a badge of honour in every arrogant gesture he made. He looked as if he regarded every female within sight as not only fair game, but a challenge to his talents, and almost instinctively Nicola lifted her chin in defiance of the challenge. From the way he kindled that slow smile again it was obvious too that he recognized the effect he had, and she started almost guiltily when Curran spoke again.

'Wasn't I right about Malinbrae?' he asked, and Nicola looked around her, giving her attention to the big hall they were standing in.

The walls were half-panelled in glowing oak, the rest matt white and reaching up to a sweeping curve of ceiling, decorated with scrolls and ornamental leaves. There were paintings on the walls, old sombre colours that had a beauty all their own, and ancient weapons, crossed in peace. It was all so exactly right somehow that she could scarcely believe it.

'It's quite an impressive heap, isn't it?' Mitchell Grant suggested, and she flicked him an uneasy glance before she nodded her head.

'It's beautiful,' she said, but addressed herself to Curran. 'It's wonderful, Curran, I'd no idea how lovely it would be.'

'I'm glad you agree with me,' he told her, his eyes glowing. 'And you fit in here so beautifully, darling.'

His cousin laughed softly to himself. 'So you do', he agreed. 'You look just right in the old ancestral home, Miss Scott.' He was not, she noticed, using the pseudo wild-west accent he had earlier, but the words were clipped and rather precise, though still unmistakably American.

For a moment Nicola met his eyes and felt the sharp jolt her heart gave when he smiled again. It was quite ridiculous the effect he seemed to have on her and she resented it, perhaps unreasonably.

'I'm grateful to you for bringing me up here, Mr. Grant,' she told him, sensing Curran's anxiety to see

16

him gone, and he smiled again.

'You're welcome, honey.'

She bit her lip over the Americanism she despised, but decided to let it ride once more. It was not worth making a fuss at this stage, and she could leave Curran to do what he would about it later.

'If you're hungry, darling,' Curran said, ignoring his cousin, 'we'll just make a quick entrance for you to meet the family, then you can go and have a freshen up before we have dinner.'

He turned back towards the room he had just left, his encircling arm taking Nicola with him, and she recalled herself hastily. No matter how she disliked this American interloper, she could not just walk off and leave him without saying a word after he had taken the trouble to fetch her.

She turned in the circle of Curran's arm and held out a hand, flinching involuntarily when strong fingers closed round it. 'Thank you again, Mr. Grant, and good-bye.'

A hint of mockery in his expression demolished her intention of appearing cool and formal, and he retained his hold on her hand for far longer than was necessary, the pressure of his fingers conveying a sense of intimacy that she found quite disturbing.

'My pleasure.' An upward glance revealed laughter in his eyes, so that she felt herself blushing like a schoolgirl and sought to free her hand.

Her fingers tingled with the strength of his grip and she instinctively rubbed them with her other hand.

'Good-*bye*, Mr. Grant.'

'You sound like you can't get rid of me fast enough,' he suggested, and smiled at the idea.

'Nothing of the sort,' Nicola denied hastily, perhaps too hastily, for she saw the dark brows flick upwards and felt Curran stiffen disapprovingly.

'I'm in no hurry to go,' Mitchell Grant assured her quietly, 'if that's an invitation to stay.'

'It isn't,' she said shortly, glaring at him before she turned back to go with Curran again.

She heard him chuckle behind her. 'So long, honey.'

Immediately she spun round again to object, only to find him already out of the door and slamming it behind him, leaving a strange feeling of emptiness in the big hall.

Curran drew her along at his own slow, halting pace and she felt her heart in her mouth at the prospect of meeting his family. She stopped as he put his hand on the door knob to open it, her eyes wide and anxious as she looked at him. 'I – I hope they approve of me,' she ventured nervously, and Curran hugged her close again.

'Father will adore you,' he promised, 'and don't take too much notice of Aunt Margaret, she isn't as bad as she appears at first sight.'

Seconds later the dreaded moment was upon her and Curran opened the door and drew her into the room beyond. It was a huge room and enough in itself to overwhelm her. The walls lined on three sides with

18

books from floor to ceiling, thousands of them, and an enormous fireplace yawned blackly immediately opposite the door.

In front of it and already smiling a welcome stood a tall, good-looking man in his fifties who could have been no one else but Curran's father, since the likeness was startling. The only difference was that in the older man there was none of the lingering boyishness that still showed in Curran's face.

He extended a hand, his eyes taking surreptitious stock of her as he gripped her fingers when Curran introduced them. 'Welcome to Malinbrae, Miss Scott,' he told her. 'We're delighted to have you.'

'Thank you.' Somewhat reassured by his welcome, Nicola was rather surprised at the different expression that greeted her on the face of an elderly woman who sat over near the high mullioned window on the other side of the room.

There was a remarkable family likeness here too, in the same brown eyes and light brown hair; hers was liberally streaked with grey, only her expression was much more stern and less welcoming than either of her menfolk.

Curran, she thought, was a little nervous of her too, and Nicola did not altogether blame him. Miss Margaret McCrae extended a large, thin hand and looked at Nicola with a steady rather disconcerting gaze. 'I'm glad you've arrived, Miss Scott, we've been waiting dinner for your arrival.'

'We don't dine very early,' Ian McCrae assured her

with a short, reproachful glance at his sister. 'Don't let my sister make you feel guilty.'

'Nicola's had no lunch,' Curran informed him. 'So I'll get Mrs. Johnston to show her her room now that she's met you, and then we can all have our meal.'

'I'm sorry you've been kept waiting,' Nicola apologized.

'Oh, no, no!' Ian McCrae begged her. 'There's no need, my dear. If anything you must be far hungrier than any of us; at least we had a good lunch.'

'Come along, darling.' Curran put an arm round her again and hobbled with her to the door. 'Mrs. Johnston will soon fix you up and then you can eat. You poor sweet, you must be literally starving to death.'

She smiled up at him as they went out into the hall again. 'I could eat the proverbial horse,' she vowed, and he kissed her gently beside her left ear.

They both looked slightly taken aback when they saw Mitchell Grant coming downstairs, a small, ironic smile on his face when he saw them. He was carrying what looked like a framed photograph in one hand and she thought she felt Curran stiffen when he noticed it.

'What have you got there?' he asked shortly, and his cousin flicked a brief glance at Nicola before answering – a glance that she would have termed warning, had the very idea not been utterly ludicrous.

'It could well have been a cat among the pigeons,' he said, tucking the object under his arm firmly. 'I've taken the lady's baggage up for her, so all is well.'

'Thank you.'

Her own brief thanks were echoed by Curran, but she felt sure that there was more behind his gratitude than there was her own, and Mitchell Grant smiled slowly. 'If you're looking for Mrs. Johnston,' he told them, 'she's upstairs.'

'I can't climb very well yet, darling,' Curran told her apologetically, 'but you can find your room easily enough. It's the second door on the left at the top of the stairs.'

'Right opposite Curran,' Mitchell told her.

She ignored the implication he managed to put into the words and answered Curran. 'I'll find it,' she said. 'And I'll be just as quick as I can coming down again.'

Curran smiled. 'Don't rush, darling,' he told her. 'Aunt Margaret can wait.'

She did not stop to explain that it was her own hunger that drove her to hurry, but went off up the wide staircase to find her room, aware that both men were watching her go. She had barely turned left at the top of the stairs when she heard Curran's voice, low and angry, and wondered how much the photograph his cousin had been carrying had to do with his sudden burst of anger.

A woman stood in the doorway of the room Curran had said was hers – a small, slim woman, whose sharp features and tight mouth were set in what Nicola feared was an expression of permanent disapproval. She acknowledged Nicola's introduction with only a brief nod of a neat grey head and led the way into the room.

Sharp dark eyes took in her appearance in one swift glance of appraisal and Nicola had the uncomfortable feeling that she had fallen somewhat short of complete approval. However, she ventured a smile, which the woman feigned not to see, and looked around the room.

It was big enough to be impressive, but with an air of cosiness too. The carpet was deep red and richly patterned with gold, exactly matching the embroidered quilt on the huge bed. Dark wood shone with the years of loving care that had gone into its preservation, and was displayed to advantage against the cool, white-painted walls. It was beautiful, and, in some indefinable way, curiously feminine.

'What a lovely room!' She walked across to the window and looked out over a stretch of garden and beyond that to what appeared to be stables or outbuildings of some sort, half hidden by trees, while as a background the vast, beautiful panorama of hills and valleys stretched mistily soft and infinite under a summer sky.

'Aye.' The sharp eyes were watching her, she knew, and something in the woman's voice made her swing round. 'It was Miss Fiona's room whenever she was here.'

'Miss Fiona?' Nicola was openly curious and suddenly uneasy. Curran had no sister, she knew, but whether he had ever had one she did not know.

It seemed the housekeeper was not prepared to go beyond that one brief reference, however, and the sharp eyes were lowered when she spoke again. The subject very obviously changed. 'If there's naught else I can get ye, Miss Scott, I'll away and see about dinner.'

Much as she would have liked to know more, much more, Nicola was forced to face the fact that no more information would be forthcoming, not from this source at least, and she wondered how much more willing to enlighten her Curran would be. 'Yes. Yes, of course.' She sent the housekeeper on her way, and remembered suddenly that the rest of the household were waiting for her to join them before they had their evening meal.

She wondered, as she hastily showered and changed, if Mitchell Grant would be at dinner. He was likely to be an unforeseen drawback to her stay at Malinbrae, and she wished Curran had warned her that he would be there.

She brushed her tawny hair until it shone, the short simple style she wore it in making her look somewhat younger than her twenty-one years. She often considered wearing it in a more sophisticated way with the idea of making herself look older, but Curran liked it as it was, and it was very little trouble to do.

A last glimpse in the mirror confirmed that the long-sleeved yellow tricel dress she had chosen looked cool and attractive and definitely did things for her colouring. It was only as she walked downstairs again that she once more thought about the previous occupant of her room, and she wore a soft frown between her brows as she considered possibilities.

The confusion of several doors opening off the hall was solved for her by the appearance of Curran and he kissed her mouth before putting an arm round her and drawing her with him into the dining-room.

Curran's father was there and Miss McCrae, but there was no sign of Mitchell Grant, and Nicola thanked heaven for small mercies. Apparently he did not live with the rest of the family, unless he had chosen merely to absent himself from this particular meal.

'Do you think you'd like living in Scotland?' Ian McCrae asked her as the meal progressed, and Nicola smiled.

'Oh, I'm sure I should, Mr. McCrae. I haven't seen much of the country yet, of course, but it's very beautiful, the little I have seen.'

He glanced at his son, smiling knowingly. 'Well, that'll be a weight off Curran's mind,' he declared, and Miss McCrae pursed her lips disapprovingly.

'If it wasn't for this damned leg I could have taken you riding in the morning,' Curran told her. 'It's the only way to see this part of the world, darling, and we haven't ridden together for some time now, have we?'

'I haven't *ridden* for some time,' Nicola told him, with a wry face. 'I'm much too lazy to make the effort when you're not around, Curran.'

'Well, as soon as I'm able I'll take care of that little

24

matter,' he promised, and smiled at her. 'You'll find it very different riding here, there's so much more room.'

'Fiona was a very good rider.'

Three pairs of eyes turned on Margaret McCrae, displaying various expressions. Ian McCrae, Nicola thought, looked embarrassed, while Curran looked oddly uneasy and flicked an anxious look at his father. Nicola was frankly curious. Perhaps, at last, she would learn who the mysterious Fiona really was.

'Mrs. Johnston mentioned someone called Fiona,' Nicola ventured, feeling that the subject was both delicate and embarrassing. 'She said the room I'm in was hers.' She looked across at Curran. 'I was curious, of course, but I didn't ask questions.'

There was a few seconds' silence, a silence that hung in the big, bright room like a shadow. It was Ian McCrae who broke it. 'Fiona McNee was the daughter of a neighbour,' he said quietly and glancing at Curran. 'She was killed last year in a car accident.'

'Oh. Oh, I'm sorry.' There seemed little else to say, for obviously Fiona McNee had been more to the McCrae family than just a neighbour's daughter, and she was beginning to suspect she knew what position she had held.

'She was also engaged to Curran,' Miss McCrae told her shortly, and Nicola felt her throat constrict as she looked at Curran for confirmation. Last year she had met Curran for the first time.

CHAPTER TWO

NICOLA felt rather uneasy now that she knew exactly who Fiona was, or rather who she had been. The big bedroom felt less cosy, and she felt sure that Margaret McCrae's manner towards her stemmed from a very real affection for the dead girl, and resentment at her taking her place.

The subject had been abruptly dropped the previous evening, but sooner or later, Nicola knew, it would inevitably rear its head again, and the prospect was not a very happy one.

Sounds of people moving about on the landing outside her bedroom door decided her that it was time she started getting herself up. It was bright and sunny again and she looked forward to her first day at Malinbrae, but she wished Curran was able to take her riding, for she was eager to see some more of the beautiful country he was so proud of.

Bathed and dressed, she went downstairs in search of breakfast, and found Curran alone in the dining-room. His father, he explained, was off on some business or other to Strathgorm and his aunt was not yet up. Nicola, however, was quite happy to have him to herself for a while and they laughed and talked as they had so often done during the last year, before Curran came north.

It was only when she remembered and casually mentioned his cousin, Mitchell Grant, that Curran lost his happy-go-lucky air and frowned. 'Father rents him the east wing,' he explained.

'Oh, I see. He doesn't live with the rest of the family?'

'Lord, no!' He looked quite appalled at the idea. 'He grubs along on his own. He dabbles in oils and he's supposed to be taking a rest from big business for a month or two.'

'Big business?'

He nodded, pulling a wry face. 'Oh yes. *He* belongs to the wealthy branch of the family. My mother's side, although you wouldn't think he had two ha'pennies to look at him, I know.'

'He looks rather as if he doesn't care what he looks like,' Nicola said, and he nodded.

'He doesn't. He doesn't have to, of course – with all the money he has he can afford to be scruffy. My Uncle James,' he explained, 'is my mother's eldest brother and he emigrated to the States about forty years ago, started a small business and made money hand over fist.'

'So Mi – your cousin *is* an American?'

Curran shrugged, already finding the subject tedious. 'Oh, he's an American all right, and with all the cockiness of his breed. There's even been a rumour from time to time in the family that his mother had a dash of Red Indian blood, but nobody's ever gone into it enough to say if it's true or not.'

27

Nicola remembered those high cheekbones and the long, lean arrogance of his body and thought it was quite possible. There was a savage kind of pride about him that made the idea quite feasible.

'You don't like him.' It was a statement, not a question, and Curran raised his brows.

'I tolerate him,' he said. 'He's not my cup of tea, but Father likes him, and it's his house.'

'Does he really paint?' she asked, and thought his answer was grudgingly truthful.

'Actually he's quite good. I've seen some of his stuff, and I have to admit he has talent.'

The conversation got no further, for at that minute the door opened to admit the man they had been talking about, and Nicola found herself subjected to the effect of that slow smile again. 'Hi!' He came further into the room and she could see that he was still dressed in casual jeans and a tee-shirt. The shirt had short sleeves and she noticed how brown and strong his arm looked.

Curran looked at him discouragingly. 'If you're looking for Father,' he told him, 'he's out.'

'I'm not.' The quizzical blue eyes rested on Nicola. 'I was wondering if Nicky would like to come riding with me. I'm just off.'

Nicola was so taken aback at the unexpectedness of the invitation that for the moment she did not even protest at the misuse of her name. 'I – I don't think so, thank you, Mr. Grant,' she said at last, and the dark brows shot upwards as he flicked a glance at his cousin.

'No?' he smiled. 'You aren't afraid of what Curran will say, are you? Curran won't mind in the least, will you?'

'I certainly will,' Curran informed him shortly. 'I'll take Nicola riding when I'm fit enough. It won't be long now.'

Mitchell looked back at Nicola and winked an eye. 'I guess *he* doesn't trust me either,' he told her, and Nicola felt herself colouring.

'You're right,' Curran assured him without hesitation. 'I don't trust you.'

'Oh, come on now,' Mitchell protested, his eyes glittering wickedly. 'I wouldn't hurt your little girl. You know me, Curran, I don't snatch babies.'

'I am not—' Nicola began, but Curran had things firmly in hand.

'Don't be so damned superior,' he told him, and Mitchell shrugged, apparently unperturbed.

'O.K. Have it your way.' He raised a hand in casual salute and lowered one eyelid again at Nicola. 'See you.' At least, she thought irrelevantly, he hadn't called her honey.

Curran looked across at her after Mitchell had gone, an anxious look on his good-looking face. 'You *didn't* want to go with him, did you, darling?' he asked. 'You weren't just staying because of me?'

Nicola shook her head. 'No, of course not. As you said, we can go when you're fit.'

He was searching her face, as if he sought something and was not quite sure what it was. 'He's right, you know, darling, I *don't* trust him, especially round you, he's too damned sure of himself and he's the type that—' He shrugged. 'Well, you don't have to be pyschic to see what he's like with women, do you?'

Nicola thought of that slow, fascinating smile and shook her head. 'I can imagine,' she said.

The first day at Malinbrae went remarkably quickly for Nicola, and she went up to bed that night feeling as if sleep had never been further from her mind. She had expended no physical energy all day and she felt that a walk before going to bed would have put her more in the mood for sleep, but she had not liked to suggest it with Curran incapacitated as he was.

Once in bed she thought yearningly of all those shelves and shelves of books downstairs in the library. A short while reading before she put out the light usually did the trick and she wished she had thought of it before she came up. As it was she lay there for some time debating whether or not to go downstairs again and hope no one heard her. There would surely be one book among so many that would suit her.

Unable to resist the temptation any longer, and more awake than ever, she slid out of bed and into her slippers, reaching for the new and rather gorgeous negligée she had bought especially for this visit. It was pale green and fastened high under the bust, with a high frilled collar that stood up all round and framed her face. She felt rather glamorous in it and felt it was a pity that there was no one to appreciate its floaty glamour except herself.

Fortunately there were no squeaky boards and she gained the top of the stairs with no more disturbance than the soft sshing of her slippers over the carpet. She found a light switch and illuminated the hall below with a soft, single light, evidently provided for such excursions, for the hall had been lit earlier by a much brighter and bigger display of electricity.

She was part way across the hall when she heard a small sound of movement behind her and spun round, her eyes wide and startled, one hand at her throat among the soft frilling of the robe. She stared unbelievingly for a moment until she realized it was no supernatural creature that had startled her but the all too solid flesh of Mitchell Grant.

He stood just inside a door hidden away under the stairs and she realized for the first time that it was probably the way through to the east wing, for Curran had told her that that part of the house was quite separate from the rest.

'Now what are *you* prowling around for in your pretty gown?' he asked softly, coming out from the shadows and smiling at her. His eyes swept over her from head to toe and she could feel the colour in her face when they came to rest on her mouth in a steady, completely shattering gaze. 'You shouldn't take such chances, honey.'

Nicola was uncertain whether to go on her way to the library or whether to go back upstairs without her book. She felt very small and very vulnerable out there in the vastness of the hall. 'I – I'm going for a book from the library,' she explained.

He nodded, another smile crooking his wide mouth. 'Can't sleep,' he guessed. 'Well, help yourself, there's plenty of them, and nobody much ever reads them that I can see.'

She hesitated only briefly, then turned her back on him and walked across to the library, and it was only when she paused to open the door that she realized he was right behind her. 'You—' she began, and he raised a brow.

'I had the same idea,' he told her, though she doubted the truth of it.

He followed her into the room and switched on the overhead light, flooding the room with light and better able to see her. 'I – I wouldn't have come if I'd known anyone else was about,' she told him, and he laughed softly.

'No, I can imagine,' he said, 'but it's really rather a shame to waste that lovely robe, isn't it? Was it bought for Curran's benefit?'

She looked at him, bright-eyed with embarrassment. 'No, of course it wasn't,' she denied. 'And you have no right to say that.'

'Sorry.'

He gave his whole attention to the shelf of books immediately in front of him and Nicola almost breathed a sigh of relief. The books in front of her were somewhat dated and rather heavy going, but she decided she would not spend too much time over choosing one, only get away as quickly as possible.

She pulled out a volume from one shelf and at the same time caught sight of an old favourite among some other classics on a shelf just above her head. She replaced the first and reached up for the other, only to find it just out of her reach.

'Let me.' He spoke from just behind her and she hastily dropped her hands. 'Which one was it?'

'It – it doesn't matter,' she told him hastily. 'Anything will do.'

'For heaven's sake,' he retorted with a trace of impatience. 'Which one do you want?'

'It doesn't matter.'

'You have some objection to my reaching down a book for you?'

'No. No, of course not.'

'Then for heaven's sake stop being so darned stubborn and let me help you,' he said, and she felt herself turn almost involuntarily and saw the half mocking look in his eyes and a trace of that slow smile on his mouth. 'Have you got something against Americans?' he asked, and she flushed.

'Not really,' she allowed, angry because he seemed bent on embarrassing her one way or another.

'But—?' he prompted.

She lifted her chin. 'They're brash and – and uncouth,' she decided rashly.

'Great! Anything else?'

He spoke quietly, but she thought she detected a gleam of something that could have been anger in the blue eyes as he regarded her steadily down the length of his nose.

'They lack – polish and – and breeding,' she went on, uncaring now that she was at last getting to grips with telling him what she thought of him, and he stood there watching her, those steady blue eyes unwavering.

'You make me feel like I should have a feather in my hair,' he told her quietly when she finished. 'Are you through?'

'You asked me,' she said, defensively, wondering suddenly how on earth she could have been so unforgivably rude to a complete stranger.

'And you told me, honey, fair enough.'

'Don't call me that!' she told him, and he raised a brow curiously.

'Call you what?' he asked.

She hesitated over the offending word. 'Honey,' she said at last. 'I dislike it.'

He said nothing for several seconds and she began to feel horribly uncomfortable as he studied her carefully, then that slow smile crooked his mouth again and he shook his head. 'I must say I have to agree with you that it doesn't apply to you,' he told her. 'In fact I guess you're just about the last girl I'd describe as sweet. O.K., so I don't call you honey. What should I call you? Nicola? Nicky?' His glance swept over her from head to toe and he smiled again. 'No,' he said, 'you're too much of a fireball for anything as mild as that – how about Sparky?'

'You could try Miss Scott,' she retorted huskily as she tried hard to control her voice.

'I guess I could,' he agreed quietly, 'but I'd rather be a bit less formal. I guess that's another American drawback, hmm? Being too friendly?'

'I – I don't object to being friendly with anyone,' she said, again defensively. 'I – I just object to people who take too much for granted.'

'Oh, you do?'

He was quiet, too quiet, and she felt that he was far more angry than he gave the impression of being. Also, she thought, with her heart hammering frantically against her side, he would probably be ruthless in his anger. 'I—' she began, feeling perhaps she should at least make some sort of apology for her outspokenness but he gave her no chance.

'If I was in Curran's shoes,' he told her in a voice softly determined, 'I'd take you across my knee and beat some good manners into you, young lady. You're too sassy by half.'

She looked up at him, half angry, half afraid of the effect of her own tactlessness. 'I – I'm sorry if I was rude.' She swallowed hard on her pride, but went on, 'I shouldn't have said so much.'

'No *if* about it,' he informed her brusquely in that clipped, rather precise accent which she recognized as his normal one. 'You were rude.'

His relentless insistence was something she had not expected and she looked at him for a moment through the thick sweep of her lashes. 'I've said I'm sorry,' she told him. 'What more can I do?'

He merely looked at her for a long minute and Nicola stirred uneasily, aware again of that underlying challenge, then he smiled slowly. 'You could take your book and go to bed like a good little girl,' he told her softly, and she glared at him. 'In fact,' he added, 'I'd strongly advise it.'

'I am not,' Nicola stated firmly, 'a little girl.'

For a moment he said nothing, then he swept her with that swift, appraising glance again and smiled slowly. 'No, honey,' he agreed softly, 'you're *not* a little girl. But you're very young and kind of vulnerable and I guess you underestimate your own chemistry, especially in that robe, and my reactions to it.'

'You're not suggesting that I came—' She stared at him in dismay, her grey eyes wide and unbelieving, although her cheeks betrayed how vulnerable she felt and she put a hand to the neck of the robe.

'Oh, not for my benefit, I'm certain,' he hastened to assure her. 'You weren't to know I was here, after all.'

'Of course I didn't!'

'But what about Curran?'

The question startled her so that she stared at him, then she tightened her hands into fists and her eyes sparkled angrily again. She was unsure just what she wanted to say to him, but it would have to be blistering in its scorn and leave him in no doubt as to how she felt about him. No matter how hard she sought the words, however, they refused to come, and frustration was added to the other emotions that churned chaotically round and round in her head until she felt she could cheerfully have hit him.

'You,' she managed at last, and a little breathlessly, 'are the most hateful man I've ever met!'

She stuck out her chin and her eyes blazed, the flimsy robe betraying the taut anger she felt, then he laughed, turning her round to face the door, pushing the book she had chosen into her hands. 'And you,' he said shortly, 'are playing with fire, honey. Now run along to bed before you get hurt.'

She went without another word, feeling suddenly as if she had somehow been too close to something she provoked without knowing it, her heart thudding hard at her ribs. He was watching her as she went out of the door and closed it quietly behind her and she heard the soft sound of a sigh released.

Curran's father proved a good host, and he seemed to have taken a liking to her. He sat with her now, on her third day at Malinbrae, in the window of the sitting-room, a room seldom used except in the very hottest part of summer when it was blessedly cool.

They had been talking about the surrounding countryside and the estate that he would one day pass on to his son. 'I suppose it's too big for these days,' he admitted with a wry smile. 'But we're very reluctant to part with any of it, in fact it would have been even bigger if—' He stopped suddenly, his face betraying the sudden embarrassment of a man who has said too much.

Nicola wondered how she could best cover the slip and save him embarrassment, but before she could think of a way he had decided that honesty was the best policy. 'You know about Curran and Fiona,' he said. 'I'm sorry, Nicola, I had intended that it shouldn't be mentioned again, but – well, my dear, you're too good a listener and I was carried away with my own eloquence.'

'Fiona would have brought another estate to join this one?' she guessed, finding the other girl's name surprisingly easy to speak, and he nodded – relieved, she thought, to have it out into the open.

'She was an only child,' he said. 'It was a tragedy she was killed the way she was.'

'It was last year, you said?'

He nodded and would have spoken, but at that moment Miss McCrae came into the room and she must have heard the last part of their conversation, Nicola thought, for she spoke without hesitation.

'Fiona died only a week after Curran told us about you,' she said, leaving no doubt as to her opinion of the matter. 'We didn't even know the poor child had been so horribly let down until afterwards.'

'You – you mean—' Nicola looked at Ian McCrae appealingly, feeling the full horror of what had happened.

'Curran broke off his engagement to Fiona only two weeks before she was killed,' he told her, obviously regretting the need to. 'But it can have had nothing to do with it, of course.'

'Of course it had, Ian,' his sister retorted sharply. 'We all know that, although you prefer to close your eyes to it. Fiona was an excellent driver and she knew that road like the back of her hand, but she was upset about losing Curran, about the shameful way he had abandoned her in favour of more immediate attractions.'

'I – I knew nothing about her, or about Curran being engaged,' Nicola said, feeling the dreadful weight of conscience on her although she had nothing to blame herself for since she had not even known of the other girl's existence. She wished Curran had been more honest about that; it would have been so much fairer to have warned her.

'Of course you didn't,' Ian McCrae consoled her, giving his sister a warning glance which she chose to ignore.

'She was such a lovely girl,' she went on, keeping the subject alive. 'And so young.'

'It must have been quite a shock to everyone,' Nicola said. 'Especially to her parents.'

'There's only her father,' Ian McCrae told her. 'That's what makes it so much more difficult for him to bear.'

'Poor Alec!' There was a suspicious brightness in Margaret McCrae's eyes and Nicola thought she understood at last the reason for her intense bitterness. She had more than a friendly feeling towards the girl's

39

father and resented any slight to them on his behalf.

The silence that fell on the room was like a shadow despite the sunny brightness outside the window and Nicola could not repress a shudder that ran through her suddenly. It seemed that Fiona McNee was not going to be allowed to fade away quietly while Miss McCrae had anything to do with it.

To her relief lunch was announced just a few minutes later and they were joined by Curran, full of some misdemeanour of one of their tenants. The meal was affable enough, but Nicola found it very hard to forget the girl that Curran had jilted in her favour. It made her feel so responsible.

She decided to go out for a short walk before dinner that evening, although Curran was rather peeved at not being able to go with her. 'I won't be very long,' she told him. 'I'd just like a little fresh air before I have my dinner.'

'You're a real outdoor girl, aren't you?' he teased, and that at least pleased him. 'I'll be glad when I can get out and about and join you.'

'So will I,' Nicola told him, and meant it. For one thing she was always so afraid she would meet Mitchell Grant when she was alone, and that made her more uneasy than she cared to admit.

He had waved a hand at her this morning as he rode across the glen to the foot of the nearest hills. He had looked incredibly small from that distance, but there had been no mistaking that tall, lean shape in the saddle astride a big grey animal that streaked across the undulating countryside like a wild thing.

She had not waited for him to come across to her, but gone back to the house and found Curran. Being alone with Mitchell Grant was something she would avoid at all costs, especially since his unforgivable jibe about her being deliberately provocative that night in the library. She would find it very hard to forgive that.

She walked down the drive from the house and along the opposite way she had come on her first time there. Out to where the road became even less passable and where the trees gave way to open moorland, opening out into a panorama that took her breath away.

She never went very far on her own in case she should lose her way, but she felt more venturesome this afternoon, also she had rather a lot on her mind after her conversation with Ian McCrae and his sister. She felt that one way to get rid of the ghost of Fiona McNee was out here on the open moor.

After a steep rise for some hundred yards or so the ground sloped downwards again suddenly and revealed a small loch, still and tranquil in the afternoon sun. It looked incredibly deep as she stood on the edge of it and she found herself absorbing some of its stillness and peace, a soft warm wind just lifting the hair from her neck so that she threw back her head to enjoy it to its fullest.

'Nicky!'

She came out of her reverie reluctantly and knew who it was that shattered her peace even before she turned her head. No one else ever called her Nicky.

He sat astride the same big grey horse he had ridden this morning and she thought how right they looked together; both animal and man had that certain primitive look about them that was disturbing, although she tried not to respond to the sudden rapid thud of her heart when he smiled at her.

'Are you lost?' he asked, and she shook her head slowly.

'Of course not. I haven't come very far.'

'No?' He looked across the way she had walked and inclined his head. 'Look back there.'

She did as she was bid and drew an involuntary breath when she saw how distant and hazy the trees round Malinbrae looked, as if they were miles away. 'I – I didn't realize,' she admitted. 'I didn't mean to come very far either, I promised Curran.'

'He'll be blowing his top if you're too long gone,' he told her. 'You'd best come back with me.'

'With you? She did not understand his meaning for a moment.

'Up here.' He indicated the saddle in front of him. 'You're not scared, are you?'

'No. No, of course I'm not scared, but it isn't necessary for me to come with you. I have plenty of time to walk back.'

He glanced at the wristwatch he wore and made a face at her. 'You have just about fifteen minutes until dinner time,' he informed her. 'It'll take you at least half an hour to get back.'

'Oh dear!' Her eyes were wide with dismay. 'Miss McCrae does hate having to wait for her dinner.'

'Then come back with me,' he insisted. 'Come on, honey, I won't eat you.'

'Don't call me honey!' she retorted, fighting some inner and inexplicable panic at the thought of riding back with him in such close proximity.

'O.K., Sparky, climb aboard, but for heaven's sake make it fast, will you, I'm getting hungry too.'

'All right, thank you.' She reached up to take the helping hand he offered and was hauled up in front of him, much too close for comfort.

'O.K.?' The blue eyes, she could see when she got closer, had a myriad fine lines from their corners and a smile showed them up even more. She nodded silently and he put his heels to the grey and sent him racing across the open country again, with Nicola clinging on as best she could.

They were almost back to Malinbrae when he slowed the horse down to a walk and looked down at her with a smile. 'You see how safe you are with me?' he taunted, and Nicola blushed furiously at the jibe.

'I never supposed I wasn't,' she retorted hastily. 'I – I don't imagine for one minute that I'm what you consider *your* type, Mr. Grant.'

For a moment he said nothing, then he looked down at her again and his mouth curled into a smile. 'Like I told Curran, I don't snatch babies,' he said softly, 'otherwise you'd be just my type, honey.'

'Don't—' Nicola began, and he laughed.

'Call you honey,' he finished for her. 'O.K., sweet-heart, but you're really too touchy, you know. It doesn't mean a thing.'

'I know it doesn't, but I don't like it.'

His mouth tightened slightly and she thought he was getting impatient with her again, as he had done the other night. 'You don't like,' he mimicked. 'One of these days, little girl, you're going to get something you really don't like and then you'll have something to shout about.' He got down from the saddle and reached up for her, his hands steel-hard round her waist as he held her even after she was on her feet. Then he bent his head and his mouth closed over hers, hard and angry and breathtaking, until he released her with a short laugh. 'Now go home, little girl, to your boy-friend.'

'You—!' She glared at him angrily, her cheeks flushed and her eyes brightly accusing.

'You hang around, honey, and I warn you—' He started to reach for her again, and Nicola turned and fled, hearing the soft, mocking sound of his laughter following her as she rounded the house.

CHAPTER THREE

IT was only a day or two before Curran decided that he was fit enough to ride again and told Nicola so. She had said nothing to him about her coming back with Mitchell in such unorthodox fashion, and certainly not that his cousin had kissed her, for she had no desire to cause open friction between the two men. It would be much better, however if Curran went with her from now on, for it would make such incidents less likely to happen.

'I think I'll give it a try this morning,' he told her. 'My leg feels O.K. at the moment, and the doctor says it can do no harm as long as I take it easy at first.'

'Oh, good, I'll be glad of your company,' Nicola said, and he smiled and kissed her.

'That's definitely decided me,' he declared. 'Come along, darling, let's go and find ourselves some horses.'

He still walked with the aid of a stick, but she thought it was more a precaution than a necessity, and he mounted easily enough. Curran always looked marvellous on horseback, and she smiled at him as they rode out of the stable yard side by side.

'There's a small, secret sort of little smile hovering round your mouth,' he told her. 'What are you thinking about?'

Nicola laughed. 'You,' she confessed frankly.

'And that makes you smile?'

'Of course, but only in the nicest possible way,' she assured him, and he reached across with one hand to cover hers.

'I love you,' he said quietly. 'I wish you felt as much for me.' He cocked a querying brow at her. 'Or do you? Is that secret little smile what I've been waiting for?'

'Not exactly,' she demurred. 'I was just thinking how – how right you look on horseback, that's all.'

He pulled a rueful face. 'Oh, is *that* all? Well, you could say that much about Mitchell.'

'And I could,' she agreed. 'He looks magnificent.'

She spoke without really thinking how rash she was being and saw him frown. 'Oh, does he?'

'Oh, Curran, you know what I mean.' She hastened to explain her meaning, not sure that she wasn't making things worse by doing so. 'He – he's so – oh, I don't know what I mean exactly. He seems so right on a horse somehow, as if they really belong together. But you must know what I mean.'

He was still frowning. 'Oh, I know what you mean,' he told her, with a hint of malice. 'I think it means you've been giving rather a lot of attention to Mitchell if you've made such close and detailed observation of him.'

'That's silly,' Nicola objected, wishing she hadn't succumbed to the temptation to pass an opinion. 'Of course I haven't studied him, it's just something that strikes you.' She looked at him from under her lashes

46

and smiled. 'Please don't spoil our first ride together by being stuffy about your cousin,' she begged.

'I wasn't aware I was being stuffy, as you call it,' he denied, and looked as if he had no intention of responding to her smile, then he turned his head and his mouth curved wryly as he reached for her hand again. 'I'm furiously jealous,' he told her, and she laughed uneasily.

'I can't imagine why you should be,' she said. 'You have absolutely no reason to be jealous.'

'You don't find him attractive?'

She looked ahead at the rolling, misty countryside and sought for the right answer. 'I'd be telling lies if I told you that,' she admitted. 'But you still have no cause to be jealous, Curran. Mitchell Grant finds me amusing, he may even find me entertaining, but I'm far too much of a – a baby for him to have any other feeling for me, even if I wanted him to. He's told me so, more than once.'

'I remember he did once,' Curran agreed, still apparently unconvinced. 'I don't trust Mitchell with any woman, whether she's supposed to be his type or not. I doubt if age makes any difference to him, he's just a natural prowler and if he sees something he likes he'll go after it, just for the sheer hell of it. I know him.'

'It sounds as if you do,' Nicola said, and looked at him curiously. It was possible he did know his cousin rather better than she could on such short acquaintance, but something gave rise to doubts when she considered his opinion. Mitchell gave the impression of being always casual and extrovert, but somehow she suspected there was an underlying seriousness behind it all that would probably make him feel very deeply if ever he did fall in love.

'You've seen what he's like,' Curran's voice brought her out of her reverie and she shook her head determinedly.

'I don't want to talk about Mitchell,' she told him. 'I want to enjoy our ride, so let's forget about him, shall we?'

The sun was warm and she lifted her face to the light wind that they created as they rode down into the glen towards that tiny loch she had discovered. The setting was idyllic and rather romantic, she thought, but then she remembered that Curran had told her the history of the place. Why was it, she wondered, that such beautiful country had been the setting for some of the fiercest fighting in history, and some of the bitterest quarrels?

'Race you!' Curran smiled at her over one shoulder before putting his heels to his mount and racing away down the slope towards the loch, leaving her yards behind and less anxious about catching up with him than about his lack of caution, with his leg still not properly healed.

'Curran! Be careful!' She followed him down the grassy, heather-patched glen towards the shining loch, but her voice was carried back on the wind and he did not hear her. Either that or he took no heed, for he continued his breakneck dash, his broad shoulders slightly forward, leaning low over the animal's neck as he urged him on. It was almost, Nicola thought, as if he was trying to prove something, and she bit on her lip when he reined in sharply and suddenly right at the very edge of the water.

He turned and grinned at her, inviting her comments, and she was tempted to think he was over-pleased with himself. 'How was that?' he asked, obviously expecting approval, and Nicola frowned.

'Foolhardy in the circumstances,' she retorted, her heart still in her mouth, for she had fully expected to see him end in the loch.

He stared at her for a moment, uncertain of her reason for being so abrupt, then he laughed and slid carefully to the ground, coming round to her, arms upstretched. 'Did you think I'd land in the loch?' he asked, and she shook her head at him.

'You might have done,' she told him. 'You took an awful chance, Curran, and you're much too big for me to have pulled you out alone.'

'Darling!' He put his arms round her as she slid from the saddle, and kissed her forehead, his eyes glowing with a warmth that tingled through her veins. 'You were worried about me breaking my neck. It would be almost worth it to have you care so much.'

'You wouldn't have known anything about it if I did,' she told him with a faint smile. 'And I wouldn't have pulled you out of the water, you know. You'd have to have stayed there until someone else came along.'

'You're a heartless little creature.' He kissed her again, his mouth hard and insistent and his arms tight about her as she fought with her own uncertainty. 'But I love you, my darling.' He kissed her again, so hard and long that she was almost too breathless to protest when he released her.

'Curran!'

'Would you really have left me to drown?' he asked softly, watching her face, a smile in his eyes as he eased his hold only a little.

'If there'd been any danger of you really drowning,' she said, 'which there wasn't, I'd have to fetch help — call out the fire brigade or something.'

'Oh, darling!' He looked at her reproachfully. 'That's much too practical a solution for an enchanting little darling like you.'

'Whether you realize it or not,' Nicola told him with a smile, 'I *am* practical. I have to earn my own living, you know.'

He kissed the tip of her nose, his flippancy suddenly abandoned, and his eyes much darker and serious. 'I know just what you are, my darling Nicola, and I love you.'

'Curran—'

'I know.' He sighed deeply and searched her face for a moment with eyes that recognized defeat. 'You're going to tell me that you haven't made up your mind about me yet, and I'm doing my best to make you see me in only the very best light. I want you, sweet Nicola, and I'll keep asking you to marry me until you finally give in from sheer desperation.'

'But that wouldn't be for the right reason, would it?' she asked, one hand smoothing back the open collar of his shirt, her gaze somewhere on the brown throat that was just above the level of her eyes.

'No, it wouldn't.' He lifted her chin with one hand and looked at her steadily. 'But you see I wouldn't really care *what* your reason was, as long as you said you'd marry me. I do love you, my darling, no matter how tired you get of hearing me say it, and I shall keep asking you to marry me because I'm convinced that sooner or later you *will* say yes.'

'You're probably right.' She smiled at him a little ruefully. 'You're very persistent and you're a very attractive man – it's a combination very hard to resist.'

'Then why resist?'

She lowered her gaze again. 'Because I'm too unsure, Curran – much too unsure to take the irrevocable step. Please be patient with me.'

He kissed her gently. 'I will,' he promised. 'I'll wait forever for you, if I have to.'

'Until I'm old and grey?' She laughed softly, her eyes soft and shining as she looked at him. 'I don't deserve such loyalty, Curran, and it makes me feel very humble.'

He smiled at her, a slow meaningful smile that reminded her rather alarmingly of Mitchell Grant so that she hastily lowered her gaze. 'I wish I had Mitchell's powers of persuasion,' he told her, and she started almost guiltily at the coincidence of his words. 'He

51

seems to have the answer.'

'Does he?' She did not look up, but studied the firm chin and rueful mouth as he acknowledged his cousin's virtues in that direction.

'According to Father, when he was over in the States last year, Mitchell was with a different woman every night and the phone never stopped ringing.' He laughed ruefully. 'I wish it ran in the family.'

She did look at him then and her eyes were gentle with understanding. 'You shouldn't wish that,' she told him softly. 'You have so much to offer a woman, Curran, perhaps more than Mitchell has, because you don't believe in breaking hearts.' It was only after she had said it that she remembered Fiona McNee, and it was too late then to take back the words.

She thought he stiffened slightly and his hands where they held her were strong as steel, the fingers digging in cruelly hard. 'Aunt Margaret wouldn't agree with you on that point,' he told her shortly, and Nicola looked up at the good-looking face set so coldly she scarcely recognized it.

'Well, I can't agree with *her*,' she said quietly. 'I don't know what happened about – about Fiona McNee, Curran, but I can't believe you deliberately hurt her.'

He still looked angry, as if he resented being reminded of her at all. 'I told her I'd met you,' he explained, his voice low and unaccustomedly harsh. 'I told her, as fairly as I could, that I'd fallen in love with you and it was no use going on. I couldn't be any fairer

52

than that, could I?'

'No, no, of course you couldn't, but—' He looked at her, a frown between his brows. 'I — I just wish you'd told me about her, Curran.'

'Would it have made any difference?'

'No, no, not to us, but I'd have been better prepared for Miss McRae's — antagonism.'

'I suppose I should have told you.' The admission was grudging, and she thought he hated making it.

'Well, it doesn't matter now. I know all about it, and I realize it couldn't have been your fault, whatever silly thing Fiona did.'

'It's only Aunt Margaret who insists there was anything other than a perfectly straightforward road accident,' he told her. 'Aunt Margaret and Alec McNee, of course. He idolized Fiona and he's never forgiven me for breaking it off.'

Nicola sighed deeply. 'I suppose it's understandable in a way,' she allowed. 'He must be a very lonely man now that his daughter's gone as well.'

He nodded, silent for quite a long while, still holding her within the circle of his arms, then he hugged her to him suddenly, his voice rough against her ear. 'You won't let it affect your judgment, will you, Nicola?' he asked. 'You'll stay on here?'

She drew away from him, drawing a line with one finger down the front of the soft white shirt. 'I won't be influenced by — by what you've just told me,' she said slowly, and choosing her words very carefully. 'But I can't commit myself to a lifetime here, Curran. Not in this same sort of — of limbo, it wouldn't be fair to anyone. I'll stay for a while, as I promised I would, then I shall have to go back and find myself another job, earn my keep again.' She smiled to soften the words. 'I'm not a lady of leisure, you know.'

'You could be.'

She smiled, shaking her head. 'Not me, Curran. If I married you, well and good, but I couldn't stay on here otherwise, you must see that.'

'I don't. No one would make any comment, I'd see to that.'

She raised a doubtful brow, and smiled wryly. 'I rather think your aunt would, for one,' she said. 'And I shouldn't blame her, Curran.'

'You know I'm willing to have you stay under any circumstances at all,' he told her, and she believed he meant it. 'And you get on with the family, don't you?'

'I get on with your father,' she agreed cautiously, 'and as long as I don't see too much of him, I get along with Mitchell too.'

He looked at her speculatively for a moment. 'Yes, you do get along with him, don't you?' He frowned for a moment. 'I wish he wasn't here. I've a good mind to get Father to send him packing if he upsets you.'

'For heaven's sake, he doesn't upset me,' Nicola told him, aghast at the idea of having Mitchell sent away for her benefit. 'And you can't even think about such a thing, Curran. He's your cousin and he has far more right to be here than I have. What's more, I certainly

54

wouldn't have anyone sent packing, as you call it, because of me. Mitchell doesn't disturb me in the least.' She wondered, even as she said it, just how true that was, but this was no time to analyse her feelings for Mitchell Grant.

'You happen to be very important to me,' Curran told her earnestly, 'and I won't let anything or anybody stand in the way of you staying on here.'

'Well, getting your cousin evicted from the east wing won't endear you to me, I can assure you,' she told him with a smile. 'So don't even think about it, Curran, please.'

He shrugged. 'All right, if you say so.' He would have preferred it, she thought, if she had been whole heartedly in favour of the idea.

She looked at the smooth, tranquil surface of the little loch and sighed. 'It all looks so peaceful out here, doesn't it?' she said. 'Which only goes to show what a deceiver Nature is. Like human nature it looks so placid on the surface, but heaven knows what goes on deep down.' She shook herself out of the mood of melancholy that seemed to have overtaken her and moved away from him. 'Come on, Curran, let's ride back before I become too profound!'

Despite his injury Curran still had his estate duties to attend to, and he did them with rather less than good grace since Nicola's arrival, for he hated leaving her for any length of time.

'I'm quite capable of looking after myself,' she assured him one morning after breakfast when he apologized for being unable to accompany her. 'Please don't bother about me, Curran. Actually I quite like riding alone sometimes, it gives me time to daydream, and this country encourages me to dream.'

Curran bent his head and kissed her cheek. 'Well, as long as you dream about me,' he warned, and smiled. 'Take care, darling, and I'll see you at lunch time.'

Nicola finished her coffee, then made her way out to the stables and saddled the little roan she was in the habit of riding. It was a lovely morning and much fresher than of late, thanks to a showery night. The roan was eager to be away and made no fuss about being saddled, flicking his ears eagerly as they left the stable yard and started down the hill towards the road.

There was no hurry and Nicola had no particular object in mind other than the enjoyment of the ride and the endless pleasure of discovering yet more facets of this ever-changing and incredibly beautiful countryside. It was so warm that she wore no jacket but relished the caress of the sun through the thin cotton shirt she wore. There was little or no wind even when they were moving, and only the very smallest white clouds overhead and drifting lazily.

She rode on past the little loch that she had visited with Curran, and went on towards where the first blue hills sat hazily on the far side. Mountains, Curran called them, but they looked deceptively small against the vast background of sky and moor with sweeps of dark pines reflecting their images in another, much larger stretch of water. Occasionally she caught a glimpse of road not too far away, winding its way towards the same blue hills, grey and dull against the patches of spiky heather and sweeping expanses of open glen.

She had no real idea what her eventual goal was, but she knew that the roan was game for any distance within reason, and that he was enjoying it as much as she was herself. The hills seemed to recede as she went on, much more distant than she had thought and she wondered if it would be wiser to go back before she went too far. There was little question of her becoming lost because she could always pick up that often-seen road and follow it back to Malinbrae.

She turned the roan and clucked him into action again, back towards the little loch that looked no more than a speck of brightness in the distance now. Relaxed still, for there was plenty of time to get back before lunch time, she was, as she had anticipated, daydreaming and perhaps not giving as much attention to the things of reality as she should have been.

Because of that she failed to react quickly enough when a small, furry, spitting creature suddenly appeared from behind an outcrop of rock right under the roan's nose. He gave a squeal of surprise and annoyance and reared, taking her by surprise so that she felt herself sliding and could only hang on grimly.

Another furious objection from the spitting wildcat, however, and the roan jerked upwards again before

Nicola had time to recover and she was hurled from the saddle with no hope of saving herself. She cried out as she fell and perhaps further alarmed the frightened horse, for, once free of her, he took to his heels and galloped off as fast as he could go in the direction his instinct told him was safety and home.

Stunned by the fall, Nicola lay for several minutes in a swirling cloud of semi-consciousness, her head throbbing painfully and her left arm numb. She had no idea, when she at last did recover herself, just how long she had been there, but there was no sign of her mount, nor indeed anyone else, and she realized with a flutter of fear that she was alone and on foot, and a very long way from Malinbrae.

She got to her feet groggily, her head swimming as she straightened up, groaning softly as she put a hand to her throbbing head. There was no one to blame for her fall but her own inattention and the instinctive fury of the wildcat disturbed at its prey. Evidence of that lay in a half-eaten bird that gaped sickeningly only a few feet away, and she shuddered. Apparently she had been sufficient deterrent for it to abandon its meal and run off.

Faced with the long walk back, she could have cried, especially as her head was still hurting and her arm throbbing now that the numbness was wearing off. She impatiently pushed back the fall of hair from her forehead and used the speck of bright water that was the loch for her guide. If she walked towards that, no matter how long it took her, she was at least heading in the right direction.

It seemed like hours, in reality it was only about twenty minutes, that she walked, and her head was beginning to spin dizzily again, so that she was forced to stop and recover. She closed her eyes for a moment, using an outcrop of rock for support, and it was when she opened them again that she saw a distant figure on horseback, riding along from the direction of the blue hills that had been her own original target.

No matter who it was she must try and attract attention, for she was rapidly coming to the conclusion that she would be unable to get back to Malinbrae unaided. Apart from the alarm it would cause Curran if she was too long gone, there was the horrible possibility of being alone and unconscious on the vast openness of the moors.

She had no idea how big she looked from that distance, or even if she showed up at all, being on foot, but she waved her arms and shouted. Not that shouting would do any good at this distance, but it gave her some release and kept back the tears that threatened.

She waved and waved and at last she thought the rider must have seen her, for she saw the horse stop and the head seemed to be turned in her direction, trying to see her better. Another frantic wave of her arms brought an answering gesture and she sank down on to the prickly heather with tears streaming down her face, her head throbbing wildly.

She must have lost consciousness again, for the next thing she was aware of was someone bending over her and an arm lifting her, a hand brushing back her hair from her forehead, gently and carefully to avoid the bump that now swelled above her right eye. The sun was warm and there was a feeling of security in the arm that held her, so that it was only reluctantly that she opened her eyes and looked up at her rescuer.

'You!'

As a welcome, especially in the circumstances, it lacked warmth, but she felt a sudden and dismaying urge to cry again, the tears rolling warmly down her cheeks as she sought for words. 'I – I—'

'Now don't try to talk,' Mitchell told her. 'Just lie right there for a bit and take it easy.'

The big grey, she noticed hazily, stood grazing peacefully just behind him and he smiled reassuringly when she looked at him again. 'I – I think I feel better,' she said, but gasped when she tried to sit upright.

'I said to take it easy,' he warned. 'You've banged your head on something, a rock, I'd guess.'

'It feels like a whole rock quarry,' she complained, her eyes closed again against the throbbing pain.

Gentle fingers touched the bump, and surprisingly were soothing. 'How come you got thrown?' he asked. 'I thought you were a good rider.'

'I am,' she insisted, despite her throbbing head. 'But a wildcat startled my horse and he threw me.'

'Another wildcat,' he smiled, and she chose to ignore the jibe. For one thing she felt far too woozy to argue with him, and that supporting arm was very comforting.

'I didn't know it was you I was waving at,' she told him, and her voice had a husky sound. She wished she could move without her head feeling as if it was going to leave her body. 'I wouldn't have called you over if I'd known.'

'And you're just stubborn enough,' he told her. 'You'd sooner lie out here and rot than let me help you, wouldn't you? You're the screwiest kid I ever came across, and you deserve to be left here until somebody else comes along and finds you.'

He got to his feet then, leaving her without the support of his arm, and she gazed up at him in sudden alarm. Surely he wouldn't, he couldn't, do as he threatened? 'You—' she gazed at him appealingly. 'You wouldn't leave me, would you?'

'No?' He was already half turned towards his horse, and she felt panic rise in her, the tears gushing down her cheeks again.

'Mitch!'

He turned back, his brows low and drawn together. 'Hmm?'

'You wouldn't – you wouldn't leave me, would you?'

'You could just be wrong, honey.' The dark face looked stern and he seemed incredibly tall from where she was. Ruthless too, if his expression was anything to go by. 'I don't like being treated like I have the plague.'

'I – I'm sorry.'

'So you're always saying,' he retorted relentlessly.

'Well, I am, I truly am.' She felt utterly, abjectly miserable and put a hand to her head, the tears running down her cheeks, blinding her so that she did not see him come down to her again, only felt the strong comfort of his arms as he pulled her against him, his hand stroking her hair.

'O.K., O.K., so you're sorry,' he said quietly. 'Now just take it easy, will you?'

'I – I'm s-sorry.'

'And stop saying you're sorry, for Pete's sake!'

'I—'

'Stop it!' He laughed softly then and held her away from him, the dark face showing a gentleness she would never have believed possible. 'Are you hurt anywhere else besides your head?'

'Only my – my arm,' she told him, trying to stem the sobs that stuck in her throat. 'My left arm, b-but I don't think it's bad.'

'Let me see anyway.' He pushed up her left sleeve and his fingers explored the soft flesh gently, watching her face as he did so. 'It's bruised,' he said at last, 'but I don't think there's any other damage. Are you O.K. everywhere else?'

She nodded. 'I – I think so.'

'Let me see your head.' He lifted the heavy fall of hair from her brow and examined the bump on her temple again. 'You took a pretty hard knock by the look of it, and you were passed out when I found you.'

'It hurts.' She sounded, she thought with a flash of

dismay, like a plaintive child, and it was no wonder he was smiling.

'Aaah! Shall I kiss it better?' He suited the deed to the word and bent his head, his lips pressed gently and briefly against her forehead, then he laughed softly and lifted her into his arms before she realized his intention. 'Come on, baby, let's get you home where the doc can take a look at you.'

'I don't need a doctor,' Nicola protested, her arms going instinctively round his neck as he lifted her. 'And please don't call me baby, I don't like it.'

'Something else you don't like,' he said unperturbed. 'The only time you haven't objected so far is when I called you sweetheart.' The blue eyes looked down at her, much too close for comfort, and their corners crinkled into a thousand tiny lines when he smiled. 'Do I gather that you don't mind me calling you sweetheart?'

'I – I—' She sought for words that were impossible to find, especially in this position with her arms round his neck and his face so close to hers that his breath warmed her cheek. 'Oh, stop making fun of me!'

She found herself watching the wide, straight line of his mouth as it crooked into a smile and a throbbing pulse added to the dizzying pain in her head. 'Making fun?' he echoed, his voice soft and husky. 'I was never more serious in my life, sweetheart.'

CHAPTER FOUR

IT had not occurred to Nicola what would happen when the roan arrived back at Malinbrae without her, and she had no idea that Mrs. Johnston, seeing the animal coming down the road with an empty saddle, immediately sent a message to Curran. He came back at once, his face pale and looking more worried than the housekeeper had ever seen him, then went out to the garage and fetched the car as the quickest way of travelling.

He had been told that the horse came back from the direction of the brae road and, guessing it would not have gone out of its way, he set off along there, watching every inch of the way for some sign of Nicola, but seeing none until he came to a turn in the road and spotted two figures moving off to the left, by some outcrops of rock. His mouth set tight when he recognized the taller of the two carrying the other.

The first Nicola and Mitchell knew of his arrival was when the strident shriek of the car's horn broke the stillness like a warning, and Mitchell turned sharply, Nicola in his arms. A faint smile touched his mouth when he saw who the new arrival was and he lifted one brow in ironic comment.

'Saved from a fate worse than death,' he joked, while Nicola bit her lip when she thought of the inevitable construction Curran would put on their appearance together.

'Please don't—' she began, and he laughed softly close to her ear.

'Don't worry, sweetheart,' he told her lightly, 'I won't give your suspicious boy-friend any cause for thinking the worst.'

'I didn't mean that,' she protested, but knew her face was bright pink as Curran made his way across the heather towards them, a frown on his face that could be seen even at this distance.

Mitchell simply stood there, holding her in his arms, a faint hint of laughter on his wide mouth and a positive gleam of it in his eyes as he watched his cousin's approach. He would really enjoy a verbal fight with him, Nicola thought wildly, and hoped he would keep his promise not to give Curran cause for suspicion.

'What the hell's happened?' Curran demanded, when he got within speaking distance.

'I had – I had a fall,' Nicola explained briefly, finding it very hard to stop herself going off into unconsciousness again.

'I gathered as much when Brownie came home alone,' he said shortly. 'What I didn't know was that you were out with Mitchell.'

'I wasn't,' Nicola insisted, and Mitchell merely raised his brows and said nothing.

'Then—'

'Mitchell came along and – and—' Her voice faltered and she felt so drowsy she had difficulty in keeping her eyes open. 'I – I didn't—'

'Nicola!' Realization dawned at last and Curran came closer, his face anxious as he looked at her. 'Darling, I didn't realize you were hurt.'

'She's got a bump on her head,' Mitchell told him shortly, 'and I'd say she was a bit concussed. She was out cold when I found her.'

'Oh, Nicola darling, I'm sorry!' Curran looked so immediately contrite that she smiled wanly.

'I suggest that instead of talking about it you do something about it,' Mitchell suggested briefly, and Curran did not even frown over it.

'I'm not very good at walking yet,' he told him. 'Could you put her into the car for me, Mitchell? I'll get her home as quickly as possible and get Doctor Bain to come and look at her.'

'I—' Nicola began automatically, and Mitchell laughed as he started across with her towards the car, his hold on her tightening suddenly. 'She says she doesn't need a doctor,' he informed Curran. 'See if you can talk some sense into her, Curran, or better still don't listen to her at all and just get the doc anyway.'

Curran ignored the advice but reached for Nicola's hand and held it tightly and reassuringly. 'Of course you need the doctor, darling, I'll call him as soon as we get back.' He walked alongside his cousin and it was obvious from his expression that he hated having to delegate the job of carrying her. 'It'll be much safer to check with him, and see if there's anything else wrong.'

66

'Her left arm's painful too,' she heard Mitchell inform him with a sly grin as her eyes drooped again. 'But I guess it's only bruised, it works O.K.'

He sat her safely and gently in Curran's car and stood back watching her while his cousin got behind the wheel and started the engine. 'Don't let her talk you out of getting the doctor,' he warned Curran, that slow smile even penetrating Nicola's fuzzy consciousness. 'She'll probably open her big grey eyes and try and make you change your mind, but don't listen to her.'

'I'm not a complete idiot,' Curran told him shortly, whirring the engine into life. 'I know when she needs a doctor, and I'll get him.'

'Ah, but you're susceptible,' Mitchell retorted, 'and little Sparky here has a great line in gentle persuasion.'

Curran glared at him, letting in the gear more sharply than skilfully. 'How would you know?' he asked, and sent the car roaring along the road without waiting for an answer, while Nicola succumbed at last to the irresistible urge to close her eyes again, her last mental picture one of Mitchell standing there at the road side laughing to himself.

'One of these days,' Curran murmured darkly, as they sped along the road, 'I shall hit him and knock some of that – that damned cockiness out of him!' He did not realize that Nicola did not hear him but was once more unconscious.

She recovered again momentarily when Curran got his father to lift her from the car and carry her upstairs,

67

and Nicola thought hazily that if her first expedition on her own had ended like this it was unlikely that Curran would be very happy about letting her go alone again.

Miss McCrae, she thought, seemed to find her being thrown no more than she had expected. Fiona McNee, Nicola thought ruefully as her head throbbed and spun, would never have taken such a tumble.

Doctor Bain, when he arrived, looked at her thoughtfully, examined her head, asked questions which she had no idea if she answered sensibly, and hummed and aahed significantly. 'It's a nasty bump,' he decided at last, surveying her over the top of his spectacles. 'And you're a wee bit concussed, young lady. You'll need to stay in your bed for a few days at least.'

'Oh, but I can't,' Nicola protested, feeling horribly tearful, while Miss McCrae, standing by, nodded her head firmly.

'She'll stay in her bed,' she told the doctor, 'if that's what you recommend, Doctor.'

'I'll call again in a day or so and see how you're getting on,' he told Nicola, as if in consolation. 'It's not too bad, I think, so you'll not be too long there. If you feel any worse, however, let me know at once and I'll come and take a look at you.'

'Thank you,' Nicola smiled wanly, resigned to her fate for the time being at least. She had a feeling that she should have felt guilty about staying in bed, for Mrs. Johnson, the housekeeper, did not exactly approve of her at the best of times. What she would have to say about fetching and carrying her meals for her while she was confined to her bed did not bear thinking about. With Miss Margaret McCrae she shared an undying admiration for Fiona McNee and looked upon Nicola as a usurper, and in some way the cause of the other girl being killed.

Curran came in to see her as soon as the doctor had gone and he perched himself on the edge of the bed, his face a picture of gloom. 'I'm sorry about this, darling,' he told her, as if he alone was responsible for her being there.

Nicola tried to smile, although she felt more like closing her eyes again and keeping them closed; it was really very difficult keeping them open. 'You're not to blame,' she told him. 'I – I shouldn't have been so careless. I'm only sorry I'm being such a nuisance.' She bit her lip hard to keep back the tears and only partially succeeded.

'Oh, darling!' He took her hands in his, his face earnest and looking worried. 'Don't cry. Of course you're not a nuisance, don't even think about it.'

'I – I can't *help* thinking about it.' Her voice quavered horribly and she felt an awful baby for giving way as she was, but there was little she could do about it.

He squeezed her hands again. 'I know you must feel pretty rotten, darling, I got myself concussed on the rugby field once, but don't cry about it.'

'I – I'm trying not to.'

'Poor darling!' He leaned across and kissed her gently beside her mouth. 'Shall I go and leave you to sleep?'

'I don't seem to be able to keep my eyes open,' she said mournfully. 'I – I just want to keep drifting off.' She looked at him for a moment, her enormous eyes bright with tears and looking very much more like a hurt child than a grown woman. 'I – I'm sorry, Curran.'

'There's no need,' he assured her, and leaned over to kiss her again, this time full on her mouth and for much longer, his eyes warm and gentle, as he spoke softly against her lips. 'I love you, my sweet.'

'I can't think why,' she told him tearfully. 'I – I've been an absolute idiot.'

'Nothing of the sort.'

'You're very patient, Curran, and I don't deserve it.'

'Of course you do!' He kissed her again. 'You rest your poor head, and when you're better we'll have the time of our lives, all right?'

'All right.'

The curtains were drawn and the room comfortingly dark, but still her head ached abominably. The doctor had left a prescription for some tablets to help it, but as yet someone had still to go for them and she felt as if every nerve in her head and neck was protesting violently. She was drifting off into the semi-conscious state again too, and as she did so she felt the tears squeeze out from under her closed lids and roll down her face.

She had no idea how long she had been in that hazy half-conscious world, but she opened her eyes suddenly with a start when she sensed someone standing beside the bed. The figure was tall and dark and the long, lean legs in tight blue jeans betrayed his identity if nothing else would have done.

'Sorry if I woke you.' His voice was low and he bent over her as he spoke so that she blinked at him hazily, still a little foggy with sleep.

'Mitch?'

'Mitch,' he echoed, and she saw the faint gleam of white when he smiled, as if he still found something to smile at even at a time like this. It did not even occur to Nicola that it was the use of his nickname that pleased him. 'I came to see how you were,' he said, still speaking softly, and bent over her with one hand on the head of the bed.

'I – I think I feel a bit better,' she admitted cautiously.

'Head still bumping?'

'A – a bit.'

'Curran's gone for your tablets,' he informed her, and smiled again. 'I offered to go for them, but I was summarily dismissed.'

'I'm sorry.'

'Your favourite phrase,' he teased gently.

She looked up at him, her eyes looking darker and big in the half-darkness, trying to focus on that mocking, inevitably amused face above her. 'I'm – I'm not up to arguing with you,' she told him huskily, and he laughed softly.

'Then don't, honey.'

'Don't—'

He laughed again, softly above her head, and she could see the glitter in his eyes as he bent his head to speak close to her ear. 'I know – you don't like being honey, do you? Well, just go back to sleep now, it's good for you.'

'Is it?' Her eyelids were already heavy again.

'It is,' he said, his voice a deep whisper. 'And I'd better go anyway or there'll be hell to pay if Curran finds me here. I sneaked up while he was gone for your pills.'

It was so terribly difficult to keep her eyes open. 'He – he wouldn't mind if – if you came to see me,' she managed, and heard him laugh softly again, one brow flicking upwards into that fall of dark hair over his forehead.

'No? You're a funny kid, aren't you?'

'I'm – I'm not a – a kid.'

'O.K., you're not a kid, you're a sexy little half-pint.' He bent over her further and his lips brushed gently against her brow. 'Now go to sleep again, hmm?'

She was almost off again, but she found herself smiling as he moved away from the bed and across the room to the door, as silently as a shadow, pausing in the doorway to look back at her.

'Mitch!'

'Mmm?'

'Thank you for coming to see me.'

She heard a faint chuckle just before he closed the door. 'You're welcome,' he told her, and was gone.

She thought for a second that she heard voices outside her door, but she was too hazy to listen and the next time she opened her eyes it was to find Mrs. Johnston beside her bed, a glass of water at hand and in the act of taking a tablet from a glass bottle.

'Oh, ye're awake, Miss Scott,' she said. 'Will ye take one of your tablets now?'

'Yes, yes, of course.'

She managed as well as she was able and was helped considerably by the housekeeper, who seemed to have a natural bent for such a task. 'Ye'd a nasty fall,' she opined, as Nicola lay back again thankfully.

'I – I'm awfully sorry about it,' Nicola said apologetically. 'I hope I won't be too much trouble to you, Mrs. Johnston.'

'Och, I don't mind,' Mrs. Johnston told her, surprisingly.

'You – you don't mind?' It must be her woolly mind, Nicola thought, that made her see that small tight smile on the housekeeper's dour face. 'But—'

'I'd always a fancy ta be a nurse,' she confided. 'I was aye keen on the idea when I was a girl, but I was no consulted, an' it was inta service wi'out askin' me what I felt.'

'Oh, I see.' It was ironic, Nicola thought hazily, that the one way she could get into the good books of the housekeeper was by being ill and having her wait on her hand and foot. While she had merely been a guest

73

and very little trouble she had not been nearly so popular.

The housekeeper tucked in the cover more firmly, and smoothed down the quilt, her eyes downcast, as dour as ever again now. 'Mr. Curran's askin' if he can come in an' see ye,' she said. 'Are ye feelin' like a visit, mebbe?'

'Yes. Yes, I think so.' It passed vaguely through her mind how different and much more formal Curran was than his cousin. Mitchell had simply waited his chance and come upstairs to see her without seeking anyone's permission, and come right into the room without turning a hair.

She put a hand to her rumpled hair and wondered how much she really felt like talking to anyone at the moment, but she had not the heart to refuse to see Curran and she smiled wanly at the woman.

'If ye're sure ye feel up ta it,' she said.

'I feel better than I did,' Nicola assured her. 'I'd like to see him, please, Mrs. Johnston.'

Only reluctantly, Nicola thought, she went to admit him and a second later Curran came in, his boyish, good-looking face anxious but smiling when he saw her. His lips brushed her forehead and she was immediately reminded of Mitchell's so similar gesture earlier.

'Hello, darling.' He shook her hands and held them tightly. 'How are you?'

'I feel better,' she told him, truthfully enough. 'Though I'm still very fuzzy. I slept most of the time.'

'So Aunt Margaret said. She looked in on you once or twice and you seemed to be fast asleep, she said.' He still held her hands and she felt the small, sudden tightening of his clasp just before he spoke again. 'Did – did anyone else come and see you?' he asked, and she knew perfectly well that he had heard about Mitchell's visit, remembering the voices she had thought she heard outside her door immediately after he left. Someone had apparently taken the trouble to inform Curran about it and she wondered who it could be.

'Yes.' There was no point in not being truthful about it, especially since there seemed little point in being anything else in the circumstances. 'Mitch – Mitchell came in to see how I was.'

'While I was gone for your tablets,' Curran said harshly. 'That's typical of him.'

'He – he was only here a few seconds, Curran, and I was half asleep. You can hardly object to that.' She really did not feel like arguing with him or even troubling to correct the impression he seemed to have of the visit.

'But I *do* object,' he insisted shortly. 'He had no right to come up here at all. He rents the east wing, the rest of the house has nothing to do with him and he has no right to go prowling about in it.'

'Does your father object to him coming into the rest of the house?' she asked, and could not have said what made her ask such a thing, he was bound to resent it. He did too, she could tell from the frown that drew his brows down.

75

'Oh, Father makes too much of him,' Curran declared, as if he resented the fact and made no secret of it. 'He seems to like that brash type.'

Brash, Nicola remembered hazily, was one of the things she had called Mitchell, so she could hardly argue with him on that point, even had she felt inclined. She remembered, too, that she had been much more virulent in her opinion and Mitchell had laughed, although she felt sure he was more touched by it than he allowed her to see.

'Darling—' Curran began, but Nicola was past caring what he had to say and had already drifted off into her shadow world again.

It was several more days before Nicola felt more like her usual self again, and her head still hurt a bit when she moved it too quickly or talked for too long. Curran came in as often as he was allowed to see her, and now that she was feeling better she welcomed his visits more. She had seen nothing more of Mitchell.

Curran sat now on the edge of her bed, his mood rather dour. 'I hope Mitchell hasn't been paying you any more sneak visits,' he said, and Nicola looked at him in surprise.

'Of course he hasn't,' she said. 'You'd have known about it, wouldn't you?'

Perhaps the jibe was unfair, but she was still puzzled about his informant and he definitely looked a little sheepish, she thought. 'I suppose so,' he admitted.

'Curran.' She stilled his fingers as they plucked at the quilt, by covering them with her own. 'Who told you about him coming up here to see me, that first day?'

He looked down at their hands. 'Does it matter?' he asked, and she nodded cautiously.

'Yes. I'd like to know.'

He looked uneasy for a moment. 'Aunt Margaret was on the landing when he came out,' he told her at last, glancing up as he added, 'and she said he was grinning like a Cheshire cat.'

'Well, I wouldn't know about that,' Nicola told him ironically. 'I was in no state to notice, and I wouldn't have thought that telling you about it achieved anything anyway.'

He shrugged. 'I suppose Aunt Margaret thought I should know that he was sneaking up here to see you while my back was turned.'

'Not exactly that,' Nicola objected, feeling as if she too was part of the suspected plan to deceive him. 'I – I suppose he was just concerned to see how I was – after all, he found me.'

'That's another thing,' Curran said, determined it seemed to make something out of nothing. 'How did he propose to get you back to Malinbrae?'

'I – I don't know.' There could only have been one way, she thought, the same way he had brought her back once before, but Curran would definitely not have approved of that.

'I suppose he was thinking of playing the big hero and carrying you back across his saddle,' he guessed.

'Perhaps.'

'Would you have come?' He looked at her narrowly

77

and Nicola began to resent the way he was making so much out of one short visit from his cousin.

'I – I don't know, Curran. I don't quite see how I could have done much else if you hadn't come along when you did. How else would I have got back otherwise?'

'I don't know, but I take a very dim view of Mitchell thinking he can take liberties with you. I won't have it.'

His humour was beginning to make her head ache again and he was doing little or nothing to cheer her up. 'I wish you wouldn't make such a fuss about nothing,' she said, a little shortly. 'I couldn't help it if Mitchell happened to be the one who came along first, and feeling as I did I didn't really care who it was came along as long as someone came to my rescue.'

'It *had* to be him, of course.'

'Oh, Curran, stop it!' She put her hands to her aching head and felt it throbbing as it had not done for a couple of days. 'My head aches and I don't want to talk any more.'

He was immediately contrite, putting his arms around her and pulling her into his arms, his hands soothingly caressing on her shoulders. 'Darling! I'm sorry, I'm sorry!' He held her tight, his face against her soft hair, his voice close to her ear.

He held her like that until Mrs. Johnston, coming in with her lunch, sent him hastily and sheepishly to his feet. The housekeeper's sharp eyes made much of the scene she had interrupted and Nicola could not help wondering if Mitchell would have been quite so easily put out or as embarrassed in the same circumstances.

It was only the following day that Doctor Bain came to see her again and declared himself well satisfied with her progress, although he suggested that she spent the rest of that day in bed and got up for a while next day if she felt like it.

There was little doubt she *would* feel like it, Nicola thought, as she lay there with a book she had little or no interest in and feeling rather sorry for herself. She had had enough of lying in bed to last her a lifetime and the sooner she could get out and into the fresh air the better she would be pleased.

Curran was busy and so was his father, so that her visitors had been non-existent, for Miss McCrae seldom came to see her now that she was better. She sat there curled up like a kitten in the centre of the huge bed, her tawny hair untidy and her mouth pursed in a pout of boredom and self-pity.

There was a brief rap on the door, then it opened a fraction of an inch and a voice called softly, 'Hi!' That brief greeting could only mean one person, but she was ready to welcome anyone who would talk to her and she wrestled with her conscience for only a moment before inviting him to come in.

The door still remained open only a fraction of an inch. 'Are you decent?' he asked, and she could not resist the laugh that bubbled up into her throat as she curled herself up into a tighter ball in the huge bed, feeling rather like a child about to do something she shouldn't.

'Of course. Come in, she repeated.

He was dressed, as usual, in rather disreputable jeans that made his long legs look even longer, and a white shirt that was opened nearly to the waist and displayed an expanse of brown chest and throat. He looked at her curled up there and smiled slowly, so that for some reason she could not quite explain she blushed like a schoolgirl and burrowed further down under the bed-clothes.

'How's the head?'

'Better, thank you. Doctor Bain says I can get up, but not until tomorrow.'

He sat on the edge of the bed, one knee raised to support his elbow, his eyes quizzical. 'You're bored.'

She pulled a face. 'I am,' she confessed. 'Curran's busy and so's everyone else, it seems. I don't like my book, and I'd give anything to be out there in the sun.'

'So you're lying here wallowing in self-pity,' he remarked with another smile, and she pouted reproach at him.

'I'm not wallowing in self-pity,' she denied. 'I'm just fed up with being in bed.'

He reached into the back pocket of the hip-hugging jeans and brought out a paperback book which he offered to her with a smile. 'Something to improve your 'mind,' he told her, and watched her face as he read the cover title.

'Oh, you—' It was a bright yellow cover with black lettering that informed her the contents concerned *America and the Americans* by Jessel Green.

'I thought it might advance your education,' he informed her, and Nicola laughed as she flicked through the pages.

'Do you think my education needs advancing?' she asked.

'With regard to Americans it obviously does,' he told her. 'Maybe you'll have a bit better opinion of me when you've read it.'

She looked at him from under her lashes, unconsciously provocative, a smile curving her mouth and lighting up her eyes. 'You think I will?'

'I hope so.'

She turned the book over in her hands, wishing there was something she could do about the ever-increasing rate of her pulse and the dizzying feeling in her head that had nothing at all to do with the bump it had received. 'Maybe your sort of American isn't covered by this survey,' she suggested.

'Bound to be,' he told her solemnly. 'I'm pretty average.'

'Oh no, you're not!' She spoke without thinking and a second later bit her lip hard when she glanced up and saw his expression.

One brow was cocked up into the fall of dark hair, and a faint smile crooked his mouth as he regarded her steadily. 'I'm not sure whether I should be flattered by that or not,' he said quietly. 'Maybe you can tell me.'

'I – I don't know either,' she confessed, and he laughed.

'You *are* a cock-eyed little devil,' he told her, and sat for a moment studying her in silence, until she could stand it no longer and stirred uneasily.

'Don't look at me like that,' she protested, her hands on her shoulders, arms crossed in front of her.

'Don't you like being looked at?'

'Not like that. You looked as if – as if you were seeing me as – as some sort of – of specimen in a museum.'

He laughed again softly, one hand lifting her chin and turning her head sideways on to him, studying her again in profile. 'Hold still,' he ordered when she tried to move.

'I won't hold still!' She managed to turn her head, and looked at him curiously, rubbing her chin where his fingers had gripped her. 'What are you doing?'

He did not answer immediately, but there was a half-smile on his lips and he seemed to be weighing up some question or other in his mind before voicing it. 'Did Curran tell you I paint?' he asked at last, and she nodded, realization dawning at last and with it a strange feeling of excitement that set the pulse in her temple hammering wildly again.

'He – he said something about it,' she said.

'I can imagine it came out as something like dabbling in oils, didn't it?' he asked, and took her agreement for granted. 'It's a hobby of mine and one I'm indulging while I'm here, though I must admit I had landscapes in mind when I started.' He looked at her again. 'Now I have other ideas. Will you sit for me?'

'I – I don't know.' She admitted to being intrigued by the idea, but Curran, she felt sure, would take quite a different view of the matter.

'You think Curran wouldn't like it?' he guessed, and shook his head. 'He won't,' he admitted, 'so it's up to you to persuade him, Nicky.'

She by-passed the name he gave her and considered how easy or otherwise it would be to persuade Curran to let her sit for Mitchell without making too much fuss about it. 'I'll – I'll see,' was all she would commit herself to at the moment.

CHAPTER FIVE

NICOLA had expected Curran to object to her sitting for Mitchell and he did in no uncertain terms. She had chosen to raise the matter at lunch a couple of days later, for two reasons. One was because she felt that Curran might be more inclined to indulge her if his father was there and possibly the older man might lend his support.

'I don't see why you object so strongly,' Ian McCrae told his son. 'It's a very good idea. If Mitch wants to paint a portrait of Nicola, let him do it, Curran. He's very good, after all, you have no fear of how it will turn out.'

'I don't object to his painting style,' Curran declared darkly. 'It's just that I don't like the idea of Nicola spending all that time alone with him.'

'Hmm.' The older man looked at her from under half closed lids, a somewhat sly look, she thought, although he appeared to be laughing too, if the expression in his eyes was anything to go by. 'I hadn't thought about Mitch and his—' a brow rose expressively, 'penchant for pretty women.' He winked briefly at Nicola and smiled. 'But I expect you can handle anything in that direction, eh, my dear?'

'I – I expect so,' Nicola agreed warily.

'You've no objection to being recorded for posterity, eh?'

She shook her head. 'No.' She looked across at Curran and met only a disapproving frown. 'I think it's quite intriguing. I've never thought of anyone like me having a portrait painted. I thought it was a privilege reserved for duchesses and such.'

Ian McCrae smiled, glancing across at his son. 'I agree with Mitch,' he said. 'Beauty is worth recording no matter who or what the sitter is.'

'Well, I don't like the idea,' Curran insisted stubbornly, and Nicola looked appealingly at his father, seeking his further support.

'I don't see how you can reasonably object,' his father said. 'Mitch is an artist, and a very good one, even if he isn't a professional, and if he wants to paint Nicola's picture how can you object?'

'Well, I *do* object.' The brown eyes looked dark and angry, but he already knew, Nicola thought, that he had lost the argument, and it did not make him any happier.

She leaned over and put a hand on his arm, suddenly feeling a little guilty about it and surprised to find how much she really wanted this picture painted. 'Curran.'

He looked at her for a moment, then smiled ruefully. 'I'm sorry, darling.' He covered her hand with one of his and squeezed her fingers. 'I suppose my jealousy is showing, isn't it?'

'Just a bit,' she agreed softly. 'But there's really no need.'

Miss Margaret McCrae at the other end of the table made a sound that could only have been a snort of disbelief and Curran sent her a brief, telling glance before looking back at Nicola. 'If you want to have your picture done, darling, you do. Actually,' he added pursing his lips thoughtfully, 'I might ask Mitchell to sell it to me when it's finished. I'd like to have a painting of you.'

'Then you don't mind?' she smiled at him.

'Oh, I mind,' he argued, 'but I can see it wouldn't be very reasonable of me, as Father says, to try and stop you. Go ahead with it, darling, and I'll come and watch whenever I can.'

That, Nicola thought, would not suit Mitchell at all, unless she was very much mistaken, but she did not say as much to Curran. Time enough to cross that bridge when she got to it.

She had never yet been in the east wing of Malinbrae and she wondered if it differed in any way from the rest of the house. It looked smaller and older from the outside and the windows as far as she could tell were leaded and not modernized as the rest of the house was.

'It was built before any of the rest of the house,' Curran told her when she mentioned it. 'It was quite a small place originally and it's been gradually added to over the years since. It hasn't been used for years until now – the east wing, I mean. Heaven knows why Father wanted to let Mitchell have it.'

Nicola could have offered the suggestion that possibly it had seemed a better idea than having Mitchell and Curran in the same house and perhaps constantly arguing, but she did not say as much.

She saw Mitchell the following morning in the garden as she was sitting in the window of the sitting-room and enjoying the sun. She was alone and quite happy for the moment. When he saw her Mitchell raised a hand in casual greeting and turned to come across towards her.

She acknowledged him, cautiously waving one hand and feeling her pulse quicken alarmingly as he came across the grass, his hands thrust into the front pockets of his jeans, and a small knowing smile on his face as he came nearer.

'Have you asked permission of your lord and master yet?' he asked, and she made no pretence of not knowing what he meant by it.

'I spoke to Curran about sitting for you,' she said. 'And both he and his father think it's a good idea.'

'Do they?' He shot a brow upwards into his hair. 'Ian I can believe, but I can't see Curran being exactly enthusiastic about it.'

'I didn't say he was enthusiastic,' she denied. 'But he thinks now that it might be a good idea. He says he'd like a portrait of me.'

He lifted a brow again, his blue eyes steady as he looked at her. 'Well, he's going to be unlucky if he thinks he's getting this one,' he told her bluntly. 'I'm doing this for myself, not Curran.'

'Yourself?' She looked uneasy, not wanting to meet his eyes, though she knew he was watching her still.

'Uh-huh. A memento of my stay in the U.K.'

'You're – you're going back?'

He did not answer for a moment and she felt bound to look up at him. When she did she saw a look that was both speculative and amused as he studied her face in silence. 'Sure I'm going back, honey, sooner or later,' he said. 'I do have a share in the family business, you know, and I'm only supposed to be taking a breather for a couple of months or so.'

'Yes, yes, of course.'

He was smiling now and his gaze was fixed disturbingly on her mouth as if it fascinated him. 'Did you think I was a fixture, Nicky?'

'No, no, I knew you weren't.' She tried hard to do something about the rapid and illogical thudding of her heart against her ribs, and put her hands together to steady them. 'When – when do you want to start painting?

'Whenever you feel up to it,' he told her. 'How do you feel now that you're up and around again?'

'Not too bad, thank you.'

'Do you feel up to sitting on a seat, and quite still, for a couple of hours?' he asked.

'I – I think so.'

'Good.' He nodded his satisfaction. 'Then we'll get started right away. O.K.?'

'Yes, of course.' She looked down at the thin cotton dress she wore and which revealed her arms and neck enchantingly. 'How – how shall I dress?'

He looked at her for a moment steadily, his eyes narrowed and concentrating. 'In that dress,' he decided after a moment or two. 'That pale green suits you and makes your hair look even more red.'

'It isn't red,' she hastened to correct him, and he smiled.

'I'm the artist, and if I say it's red, then it's red,' he told her. 'But actually it's a kind of tawny gold-red colour.' One hand reached in through the open window and twined a finger in the softness of her hair. 'It's beautiful, Nicky, like the rest of you.' His voice was deep and soft and she felt an involuntary shiver trickle along her spine.

'I'll be with you in about ten minutes,' she told him. 'If that's all right.'

'Fine,' he agreed, inclining his head, and started off across the garden again, turning after he'd gone only a few yards to call back to her. 'Oh, incidentally, I don't like being watched when I'm painting,' he told her. 'So warn Curran he can't come and hold your hand, will you?'

She nodded, feeling her cheeks pink and remembering what Curran had said about coming to sit with her. He wouldn't take kindly to the idea of his exclusion and she would have to be very careful how she worded it.

As luck would have it he came into the room just as she was going upstairs to tidy her hair, and he frowned crossly when she was obliged to mention that he would not be welcome while she was doing her modelling for Mitchell.

'He can't stop me,' he said, when she told him. 'He doesn't own the place.'

'But he does rent the east wing,' Nicola pointed out to him. 'That gives him the same rights as an owner in that part of the house, Curran. You can't very well come unless he invited you.'

'Which he won't,' Curran retorted, his brown eyes dark with anger. 'Not when he has the chance of having you to himself. Well, he can think again – I'm going to sit with you and he can do what the hell he likes about it.'

'No, Curran.' Nicola surprised even herself with her firmness and Curran stared at her unbelievingly.

'You – you mean you side with him?' he asked, aghast at the very idea.

'I don't side with anyone,' she denied. 'But I'm beginning to feel that you don't trust me either when you insist on coming with me, and I am to be trusted, no matter what you think.'

'Oh, darling, of course you are.' He took her hands, his boyish, good-looking face contrite. 'I'm sorry you got that impression. I had no intention of blaming you.' He still looked unhappy about letting her go alone. 'I just don't trust Mitchell. I *know* him.'

'And you know me,' Nicola insisted. 'Please don't treat me like a small child incapable of looking after herself, Curran. I can cope with Mitchell if I have to, but I'm sure all he's interested in is painting my portrait. Anything else is far from his mind.'

'Huh!' Curran snorted his disbelief. 'You *don't* know him very well!'

'I know him well enough to recognize the warning signs if they appear,' she informed him, losing patience. 'Now please let me go, Curran, and don't make any more fuss about it.'

The first thing that struck Nicola about the east wing after she had gone through that little door under the stairs where Mitchell had surprised her that night was that it seemed so small and almost cottagy after the vastness of the rest of Malinbrae. The ceilings were lower and altogether it had a much cosier feeling about it. It obviously lacked the attentions of Mrs. Johnston, but it was clean enough and moderately tidy, and she wondered if he also did his own cooking.

She had peeped into two small rooms in search of him when he appeared from a door right at the far end of the corridor, rubbing his hands on a piece of rag that had certainly not seen a wash tub for some time. He smiled when he saw her and called her on with a waving hand from the doorway.

'Come on in,' he told her. 'It's not much, but it's home.'

She followed him into a room that surprised her with its size, although the ceiling was low here as in the other rooms she had seen. 'It's bigger than I expected,' she admitted, and he laughed.

'This room is,' he told her. 'It's two knocked into one and this is where the work's done.'

Canvases stood propped against all the walls and at one end a big window gave bright sunlight to the whole room almost. There was very little furniture, but an old armchair and a sort of couch, also littered with canvases. An easel stood up nearer the window with the usual paraphernalia of artists around it and a long cushioned seat ran the whole length of the window.

He watched her as she walked the length of the room, and smiled when she turned. 'Did you have any trouble?' he asked, and she shook her head.

'No, of course not.'

He laughed softly, still rubbing his hands on the rag. 'Liar,' he told her, and laughed again when she flushed. 'I've been trying to get the exact colour of your hair by experimenting from memory,' he said, 'but it isn't easy.'

She swung the heavy silkiness of her hair experimentally, almost unconscious of the provocation of the gesture. 'Is it so difficult?' she asked, feeling suddenly and dismayingly nervous now that she was alone with him in this old, remote part of the house.

He came closer and, without warning, grabbed a handful of her hair, a smile on his face as he looked down at her, with the protest already forming on her lips. 'Everything about you is difficult to capture,' he said quietly, his voice deep and suddenly more vibrant. 'I shall enjoy the challenge of you, honey.'

'Don't call me—'

'Honey,' he finished for her, and tugged sharply at the hair he still held. 'You sit down on that window seat, little one, and don't start going Limey on me already.' He took her arm and led her across to the window, sitting her down in one corner of the seat, lifting her right arm to rest on the wide sill.

He turned her face to look out of the window and then stood back, studying the picture she made and apparently dissatisfied with it after several minutes' consideration. 'No,' he declared at last, a little impatiently. 'It isn't you. It's too – too still, too prissy.' He strode round the room watching her from all angles and she dared not move except to follow him with curious eyes. 'There's a certain way you look, a way you have of holding your head, that's what I want to get.'

She waited patiently, knowing he saw her as no more than a part of a picture he was trying to create. 'Something a bit more—' He shook his head impatiently. 'It's no use,' he declared suddenly, 'not while you insist on looking like some prissy little miss from way back.'

Nicola flushed, rising to the bait inevitably. 'You don't have to be so rude,' she complained.

'I wasn't being rude,' he told her, 'just stating a fact.'

She turned her head and glared at him, her eyes huge and sparkling, her chin angled defiantly, and he laughed. 'That's it, honey,' he told her, his hand flying swiftly across the virgin whiteness of the sketch pad on the easel, the black lines taking shape almost miraculously. 'Keep it up, that's just the look I want.'

She stared at him huge-eyed. 'Do you mean you—'

He was still laughing and sketching busily. 'Lift your chin a little higher, honey – come on, a little higher.' He smiled as he sketched. 'That's my girl!'

'Oh, you're an – an ogre!' she declared, unable to resist a smile for the way he had taunted her into looking as he wanted.

'I should have you outside in the open,' he told her, and looked up at her with a quizzical gleam in his eyes. 'Will you come?'

'Outside?' She looked uncertain and felt more so, wondering what Curran would have to say about this new move. 'Where exactly?'

'On the moors, where else?'

'You mean—'

'I mean where I can get a background that suits you,' he said. 'Down in the glen, as the song has it. All that heather and water and with the sun on your hair you'd be enough to inspire anybody, let alone a budding Gainsborough like me.'

'Are you serious?' She looked at him, sensing some of his feeling for the idea, but quite certain it could only lead to further objections from Curran.

'Of course I'm serious,' he assured her, and there was a gleam of challenge in his eyes when he stopped work for a moment and looked at her directly. 'Will you come? Do you feel up to it?'

'Oh, I feel up to it, of course I do,' she told him. 'After all, I'm not required to do anything except sit still, am I?'

He made a face, his eyes still watching her for reaction. 'I had thought something a little more mobile might be a good idea,' he informed her, and she looked puzzled. 'You know, kinda moving about while I catch you in your infinite variety.'

'You're very fond of quoting today,' she said, her heart doing strange things at the thought of being out there on the moors with him, having him watching every move she made and recording it.

'Maybe,' he conceded, giving little thought, 'I guess I'm a little short on ideas of my own in the circs. Now will you come out there with me, or are you scared of the idea?'

'Not at all.' That may not have been strictly true, she thought, for he was a force to be reckoned with, no matter even if she had told Curran she could deal with anything he did.

'Over near the loch?' he suggested softly, his blue eyes glinting wickedly, probably because he was already anticipating Curran's inevitable objections to the idea.

'The little loch?'

He nodded, folding the cover over his sketch pad, and getting to his feet, ready to be away right now, anticipating her acquiescence. 'Do you need a coat?'

She shook her head. 'No, I don't need a coat, it's much too warm, but I think I ought to let Curran know where I'm going.'

He shot a brow up into the fall of dark hair on his forehead. 'Why, for heaven's sake? You know he'll only read something into it that isn't there and raise an almighty shine about you coming. Worse still, he'll probably want to come with us, and that'd ruin the whole thing.'

She looked at him suspiciously, made more uneasy by his choice of words. 'I don't see how having Curran with us could ruin anything,' she denied. 'You'd have the same background and the same model, you might even get that expression you're looking for.'

He shook his head and smiled slowly. 'Not with Curran around I shan't,' he stated definitely. 'He'd get in my way.'

'Get in your—'

He grinned maliciously. 'Like I said, sweetheart, I don't like being watched while I work, it ruins my concentration, and if you're going to insist on Curran tagging along as chaperon to your maidenly innocence, then we may as well stay home and forget the whole thing.'

Nicola looked at him, horribly uncertain what she should do. If Curran came with them, always providing he was free to do so, he would inevitably quarrel with his cousin and, while Mitchell would probably take the idea in his stride, she did not feel like playing peace-maker for the rest of the day.

'I think he's gone out,' she said, a small frown betraying her indecision. 'So perhaps if – if I just leave a message for him it would be all right.'

'O.K., do as you please.' He stood with the sketch pad under one arm, a smile on his face as her waited for her to make up her mind. 'But don't be too long, honey, I'm not a very patient man.'

Nicola tossed her tawny hair, her eyes bright with the realization that he was awaiting her pleasure. 'I've noticed that,' she told him. 'But if you're going to have me for a model you'll have to learn to *be* patient. I like doing things in my own good time.'

'I'd noticed *that*,' he said quietly, watching her as she left her seat by the window and came across the room towards him, deliberately taking her time. 'Step on it, will you?'

'I'm not rushing around and getting a headache just to please you!' Nicola retorted, and saw his mouth crook into a smile as she passed him.

He said nothing, but as she went past a heavy hand reached out and slapped at the last part of her anatomy out of the door, and she went through into the main part of the house with the sound of his laughter following her.

There was, as she had expected, no sign of Curran, and Mrs. Johnston informed her that he had just left for one of the crofts. Nicola, after some hesitation, left a message for him with Miss McCrae, who pursed her lips knowingly when she told her where she was going, but made no comment beyond a brief nod and a murmured, 'Very well, Nicola.'

Nicola returned to the east wing, but found Mitchell waiting for her on the drive outside, tapping an impatient foot. 'You finally ready to go?' he asked, but she refused to be drawn and walked with him along the drive and out on to the road.

She said little as they went because she felt gauche and rather shy suddenly now that they were on their way, and she already wished she had not come so readily. He was a most disconcerting man and she wondered if she had been too rash in coming out alone with him.

They left the road soon and walked across the soft springiness of the turf and heather, and, as always out here, she soon lost any other feelings she had, lost in admiration of the sheer beauty and grandeur of the scenery. Those huge expanses of open glen seemed to suit her every mood and she thought, judging by his expression, that her companion was affected in much the same way.

The loch shone like a sheen of silver in the sun and there was a hint of mist still around the foot of the distant blue hills. The air was warm and promised to become warmer as the day wore on, and the stillness was almost tangible. It was a perfect day.

'It's so incredibly beautiful,' Nicola breathed, as they drew nearer the loch, and he looked down at her and smiled. That slow, inviting smile that did such wild things to her pulse despite her resolution not to allow it to.

'Now you have the look I want,' he told her softly.

She hastily lowered her eyes. 'I – I didn't know I was looking any special way,' she said, and he laughed softly.

'You look like you just had a glimpse of paradise,' he teased gently, and forestalled the words that rose to her lips. 'You just sit there by the loch, honey, and take it all in. Let your eyes shine like they are now. I'll do the rest.'

She looked at him, unsure again, and gathered a small frown on her brow. 'I – I wish I knew exactly what it is you want of me,' she said. 'I'm not used to – to doing this, and—'

'And you feel all shy and nervous,' he guessed softly.

Nicola raised her head, suspecting sarcasm. 'You think I'm silly and affected, don't you?' she demanded, on the defensive, and he did not answer for a moment.

'I think you're very, very beautiful,' he told her at last, one hand lifting her chin. 'And I only wish—' He shrugged, his smile ironic as he released her. 'Let's get down to some work, shall we?'

'You work,' she retorted, trying to still the pulse his touch had sent racing. 'I'll just sit and admire the scenery.'

She did just that, right at the edge of the loch, with its rippling silver making a background for her, and the misty blue hills rising behind it all. It was idyllic and, she thought hazily, should be shared with someone very special.

Unconsciously she looked across at the tall, self-possessed and rather overpowering American who could make her feel so unsafe for no reason at all, and she got to her feet, suddenly restless. He made no attempt to stop her, or complain of her changing her position, but merely followed her with his gaze and continued sketching busily.

Some of the heather was showing colour and she bent and plucked a sprig of it, twirling it between her fingers as she walked on. She had wandered only a short distance, however, when he called her back, peremptorily and with no thought that she would do other than obey.

She turned and looked back at him, at the dark head bowed over the sketch pad and the strong brown arms bare to the sun and in such contrast to the pale blue shirt he wore this morning. For a moment she defied his instruction to come back, and stayed where she was long enough to let him know what she was doing, then he looked up at her again and held her gaze.

'I can't see you right over there,' he called out. 'Come back here, where I can see you.'

'I'm coming,' she replied, in no hurry to comply.

'In your own good time, huh?'

She smiled, swishing her sandalled feet through the prickly heather, walking slowly and almost unconscious of the provocative swing of her hips, a realization that would have appalled her. 'Now am I near enough?' she asked, and looked across at him, lashes half concealing her eyes.

'Fine.' She did not altogether like the look of the smile he wore. 'Hold it there for a couple of minutes, will you?'

He sketched busily, and she watched the way his

hands moved over the pad. So quick and sure, wondering if he ever did anything without knowing exactly what he was doing.

In the warm sun she began to feel rather drowsy and her head was beginning to ache a little too, although it was not too bad as yet. Perhaps she had been rather rash to come so far after being inactive for so long. It was only a couple of days since she had come downstairs for the first time and it was quite a long walk from the house out here. The sun too, was very warm.

'Nicky!'

She opened her eyes wide in startled surprise at his cry and saw him coming towards her, the sketch pad abandoned, a look of anxiety darkening his eyes as he knelt beside her.

'Nicky!' He took her hands and held them to his chest so that she could feel the strong, steady beating of his heart under her fingers. 'Are you all right?'

She looked up and smiled. 'I felt sleepy,' she confessed, and he made a face at her ruefully.

'Do you mean to say you were just cat-napping? I thought you were passing out on me, for heaven's sake.'

He seemed almost disappointed, she thought, and did something to remedy that. 'My head aches a bit,' she told him, looking up through her lashes at the reaction that brought.

He immediately looked anxious again. 'And I let you sit out here in the sun,' he said, and moved so swiftly she had no warning of his intention, but squeaked surprise when she was lifted into his arms and carried over to where a couple of scrub-like trees converged to create a patch of shade.

He laid her down gently and sat beside her, his long legs curled under him, one hand on her forehead, the other holding hers. 'I'm all right,' she insisted, wondering if she had given him too bad an impression, but he still frowned.

'You've been sick for a week or so and only up and about a couple of days,' he said, bent on taking the blame, apparently. 'And here I have you sitting out in the sun with nothing on your head.'

The anxiety was both unexpected and disturbing, but she felt he was behaving rather as if he was entirely responsible for her welfare. As if she was not capable of making her own decision to come out here with him.

'It was as much my fault,' she told him. 'I'm quite capable of deciding whether I came out or not.'

'Maybe,' he allowed doubtfully. 'But I'm old enough to know better than let you do it.'

'Oh, for heaven's sake!' Nicola declared indignantly. 'I'm not a five-year-old child. Stop talking as if I was some – some baby you're supposed to be looking after!'

He looked at her steadily for a moment, then, to her chagrin, burst into laughter, hugging her to him so that it took a while to struggle free of him. 'Oh, honey, you're wonderful, you *really* are wonderful!'

'Will you stop laughing!' She leaned away from

him, her eyes bright with anger, the colour high in her cheeks. 'Stop it, Mitch!'

He looked down at her, laughter still in his eyes. 'You think I'm baby-sitting?' he asked.

'You sound as if you think so.'

He laughed again, and she refused to let him hold her hands. 'For Curran, maybe?'

'I don't care who for,' she said, seeing herself rapidly getting the worst of the exchange. 'I object to being treated like a five-year-old.'

'You object?' His gaze slid over her face and came to rest on her mouth, and she thought he was growing angry himself. Certainly there was something beside amusement glittering in those dark blue eyes and it made her uneasy. 'Honey, you object to more things than any gal I ever knew.'

'Maybe the sort of women you're used to don't object to *anything*!' The retort was impulsive and rash and she knew he would never let her get away with it even before she had finished speaking.

His hands on her shoulders had a hard, angry strength as he pushed her down into the prickly embrace of the heather and his mouth found hers with a kind of savagery that stopped her breath, making the throbbing in her head turn to dizziness.

He held her there for what seemed like forever, the unrelenting strength of his body making resistance impossible, even had it entered her head. Then suddenly she was free and he was sitting up beside her with his right hand running through his hair, an expression on his face that she could see only in profile. It was an expression she found impossible to interpret.

After a moment she sat up too, putting a trembling hand automatically to her hair, a soft uncertain look in her eyes. There was nothing she could say, nothing she wanted to say. She had recognized the challenge he represented the very first time she had met him, and she had known that sooner or later she would have to face a moment like this.

Without turning round he spoke, quietly and without much expression, in that clipped, precise way of his. 'You'd better go back to the house,' he told her briefly, and Nicola stared at him for a moment uncomprehendingly, trying hard to steady her voice and sound matter-of-fact.

'You haven't done much sketching yet.'

'I've done quite enough for one morning,' he told her shortly, still keeping his gaze steadily ahead. 'I guess we both have.'

It was difficult to know what to say next. She could simply get up and leave him, or stay and fight the growing awareness that stirred in her, go on as if that brief lapse had meant no more to her than it had to him.

'I'm – I'm not blaming you entirely,' she ventured, and he turned his head briefly to look at her, his gaze curious, almost speculative, then he looked away again hastily when she met his eyes.

'Aren't you?'

She bit her lip for a moment before finding words. 'I

– I mean I—' etti returned loftily. "And thought I knew that Dirk would like to make a nuisance of himself. I

– I mean I—'

'I know what you mean!' He sounded impatient and she felt herself draw back, her hands tight together, although whether his impatience was with her or himself it was difficult to guess. 'I don't like acting out of character, Nicky.'

'I didn't know you were.'

Again he turned and looked at her briefly, a small tight smile touching his mouth. 'I don't normally behave that way with little girls,' he said shortly.

Nicola felt the colour in her cheeks and clenched her hands even tighter, growing angry at his determination to make her appear the injured innocent. She had known at the back of her mind that he would react as he had to her taunt and she disliked being treated as if she was childishly naïve, and been taken unaware.

'Because you did something you're sorry for,' she told him, tight-lipped but determinedly cool, 'you don't need to be so rude to me.'

He turned again and a wry smile crooked his mouth as he looked at her. 'No, I guess I don't,' he admitted, his voice low. 'I'm sorry. Just the same, Nicky, I'd rather you were anywhere but here at the moment. I don't like breaking my own rules and I need time to take a breather on my own. O.K.?'

'Mitch—'

'*Please*, Nicky!' He shook off the hand she had placed on his arm, his smile firmly in place as he looked up at her, now on her feet. 'Go way, li'l girl, you bother me.'

'Ooh, you—!' Nicola turned her back on him, running back through the heather, her hands tightly clenched against her breast, a suspicious shine in her eyes. It was only when she had walked almost all the way back to Malinbrae that she realized *she* should have been the one making most fuss about it, not Mitchell.

CHAPTER SIX

It would have been difficult for Nicola to say just what her reaction was after she got back to Malinbrae. She could not truthfully say that Mitchell's kissing her had been completely unexpected, but what had surprised her was her own compliant reaction to it at the time. She should have felt angry, maybe even a little ashamed that she had allowed things to get so out of hand, but instead she had felt only pleasure and a dizzying sense of excitement, so that she had offered not even a scrap of resistance at all. Curran, if he ever knew, would be furious.

She said nothing, of course. She could not entirely blame Mitchell for the incident and letting Curran know could only result in a quarrel between the two men. Whether or not her portrait would ever be completed remained to be seen, but she would be very disappointed if it wasn't.

Curran, naturally enough, was curious to know how they had progressed, and he seemed quite resigned now to the idea of her sitting for his cousin. They were walking in the garden after dinner, and he seemed in an unusually jocular mood after his display that morning.

'Has he made a start yet?' he asked, and Nicola juggled with her thoughts before she decided how much to tell him.

'He's only made some preliminary sketches yet,' she informed him. 'All the best artists do, I believe.'

'I wouldn't know about that.' He sounded as if he cared even less. His interest extended only as far as her portrait and its progress.

'We – we went outside to do some of the sketches,' she told him. 'Did Miss McCrae tell you?'

He looked at her curiously, and she wished now that she had not told him. 'No. And I don't see why you had to when he has a perfectly good studio there.'

Nicola shrugged, hoping to dismiss the subject as lightly as she could. 'Well, he seemed to want some outdoor background and I saw no reason to disagree.'

'Where?'

'On the moors. By the little loch, actually.'

He frowned and she sighed inwardly. 'That far away? What on earth for?'

'I told you, for background; it seemed reasonable enough to me.'

'It would,' Curran retorted shortly. 'You don't know him like I do.'

'So you're very fond of telling me,' Nicola retorted. 'And I wish you'd stop being so suspicious.'

He sighed, remembering her accusation that he didn't trust her either. 'I'm sorry, darling, I forgot.' They walked down the wide gravel path, his arm around her shoulders, her head not reaching his shoulder.

'That's a lovely big studio,' she ventured, trying to get things back to normal. 'Much bigger than I expected.'

She had the feeling that he was considering what he said next very carefully, and he sounded rather hesitant when he spoke. 'It was made as a studio,' he said at last, and Nicola looked at him curiously, wondering why such a simple matter should have given him cause for thought.

'I guessed as much,' she told him, 'from the window. Was it made specially for Mitch?'

His hand on her arm, she thought, tightened imperceptibly and he looked down at the smooth greenness of the grass edging the path rather than at her. 'No.' She could feel his arm taut around her shoulders and wondered what caused it, although some small, niggling doubt was already in the back of her mind. 'You – you know about Fiona,' he said then.

'Yes, I know about Fiona.' She spoke quietly, and wished she need not experience that odd feeling of coldness in her stomach at the mention of the dead girl.

'When – when we were going to – to be married, Father had the east wing prepared for us.'

He sounded stilted and oddly unlike his usual self, and she faced the fact for the first time that he had been much nearer to marrying Fiona McNee than she had realized. It was not easy, but she was determined that she would not be touched by the tragedy of the other girl's death. She was part of Curran's past and as such she must remain just that. Nicola had had nothing to do with her being killed and neither had Curran. Just the same she shivered involuntarily, although the evening was warm still.

'Was Fiona an artist, too?' She sounded quite casual, she hoped, and Curran smiled.

His smile was indulgent and it was not difficult to imagine him teasing the other girl about her dabbling, as he would inevitably call it. 'She liked to try her hand at it,' he said, 'but she wasn't really an artist. Her father's good and Fiona was always trying to emulate him, but not very successfully. They were always very close, she and her father.'

'Poor man!' Her sympathy for Alec McNee was genuine, but Curran seemed not to notice; he was still dwelling on his own father's reasons for having the studio built.

'I think Father had the studio made more because he liked to spoil her than because she had any talent much.'

'Oh, I see.' They walked in silence for a while, the sun gradually going down behind the hills and bathing the whole garden in a blood red glow. She could see so clearly Curran and this girl she had never really seen, planning their home together, making it just as they wanted it, with a studio for Fiona to indulge her taste for painting. It was a picture she found ever harder to dismiss.

'Everyone seems to have been very fond of her,' she ventured then.

'They were.' The reply was brief and somehow revealing and she looked at him sharply.

'Curran, do you – do you ever regret – doing what you did?'

She was not really surprised when he did not reply at once and in the negative, for he seemed to have left her for a world of his own suddenly. 'No,' he said at last. 'I don't really regret it, Nicola. How can I when I have you? But I wish it could have been different. That she need not have died. I mean – it makes me feel guilty sometimes, and I don't like that.'

'I rather thought,' Nicola told him quietly, 'that *I* was being held the guilty one. Your Aunt Margaret thinks so, at least.'

Once again he hesitated before reassuring her. 'Oh, don't be too worried by what Aunt Margaret does,' he told her, after a moment or two. 'She sees it all from Alec McNee's side, you see. She's been in love with him for years.'

Put so bluntly it sounded callous and rather cruel and Nicola frowned over it. 'I thought she must be fond of him, from the way she spoke,' she said.

'Actually if it hadn't been for this business with Fiona,' Curran told her, 'I think Alec would have asked her to marry him. Now, of course, he's not very enamoured of any of the McCraes, although there's been no real quarrel.'

Poor Margaret McCrae, Nicola thought ruefully. No wonder she appeared so bitter and resentful about Curran's change of heart. The resentment was only in part for Fiona McNee, the rest was for her own shattered hopes. How she must hate being obliged to play hostess to the girl she held responsible for her unhappiness!

'Whatever happens,' Nicola said, 'I can't altogether blame your aunt for feeling the way she does about me.'

He hugged her close suddenly and kissed her cheek. 'Oh, she'll come round eventually,' he told her. 'When she knows I'm quite definite about marrying you.'

His answer brought her own position back to mind and she frowned over it for a moment. 'I – I wish you wouldn't be so certain I *will* marry you,' she said, and he laughed, apparently in an optimistic mood suddenly.

'Oh, you will, my darling, because I love you.' Again she could see Curran with his arm round Fiona's shoulders, walking in this same spot, perhaps even using the same words, and she shrank from it, suddenly afraid of nothing she could put a finger on.

'You promised you'd give me time,' she reminded him, in sudden panic, and he hugged her close again.

'So I will,' he promised again. 'But you will say yes eventually, my darling, because I shall lay siege to you until you do.'

He brought them to a halt, his hands on her shoulders, his good-looking face so boyishly earnest in the evening light, then he pulled her close and his mouth sought hers, gently at first, then with a demanding hardness that made her stir uneasily and move her head. His lips pressed warmly on to her neck and throat and he buried his face in the softness of her tawny hair. 'I love you,' he whispered harshly. 'I love you, Nicola, and I'll never let you go.'

It was almost with relief the following morning that Nicola learned that Curran had left early on some business to do with the estate and would not be back until evening. She needed time to think and she could not with him in such close attendance.

She wondered if Mitchell was expecting to see her that morning, or if he had had second thoughts about the picture after yesterday. Really, she thought wildly, her life was becoming more and more complicated the longer she stayed at Malinbrae!

She hesitated to go through into the east wing and see if she was expected, but Miss McCrae's silent company drove her to it eventually and she went through the little door near the stairs with a strange feeling of excitement stirring in her heart.

The doors of all the rooms were closed, except the studio at the end, and she walked along the passage wondering if she should give some warning of her approach. She could hear nothing and there seemed to be no one about. Perhaps Mitchell was not even up yet; it was quite early by some standards.

She peeped round the edge of the studio door and found it empty, going further in when she caught sight of something on the easel that she had not seen before.

Soft-footed, she went across the room and looked closer at it, her heart beginning a rapid and anxious tattoo when she looked at the portrait propped up on the easel.

It was a very good picture, beautifully executed and obviously painted by someone who loved the subject, for there was a soft radiance about the small oval face that spoke of trust and understanding. Big dark eyes looked half shyly from under heavy lids fringed with dark lashes and a wide, smiling mouth gave the face character.

Nicola smiled to herself as she looked at it, and wondered who she could be. Probably one of Mitchell's earlier conquests, for she was only young and he had declared himself not a baby-snatcher. Perhaps he had been trying to capture something of her expression to give him the look he wanted from Nicola.

She looked at it for a long time and did not even hear Mitchell come into the room until he spoke just behind her and made her cry out in alarm. 'Who's your friend?' he asked.

Nicola looked at him for a moment, suspecting that he was teasing her, then she looked back at the painting again and a sudden coldness contracted her heart. 'I – I thought it was yours,' she said.

He came and stood beside her, eyeing the picture with a professional as well as a curious eye. His dark face had a stillness that she had seldom seen there and a tightness about the wide mouth that was like a warning. Only she could not think who for.

Then he picked up the canvas and turned it over, looking at the back, his mouth contracting further as he put it down on the floor against the wall. 'I'll return it to its owner,' he said shortly, and Nicola blinked at him.

'It's—' she began, but swallowed hard on the name.

'It's Fiona,' he said quietly. 'And if this is Curran's idea of being funny—'

'Oh no,' Nicola said swiftly, 'he wouldn't do a thing like that. Not with – not about Fiona.'

He pursed his lips for a moment thoughtfully. 'No,' he admitted at last, 'I guess he wouldn't. It must have been you know who.'

Nicola frowned curiously. 'Do I?' she asked, and he smiled wryly.

'You must have noticed that Aunt Margaret isn't your greatest fan, honey, haven't you?'

Nicola looked appalled. She knew Margaret McCrae disliked her, perhaps felt even more strongly than dislike, but that she would do something as underhand as this took her breath away. 'You don't mean that Miss McCrae put that painting here?' she said. 'Oh no, Mitch, you must be wrong, surely.'

He looked at her for a moment, his hands on her shoulders, as if debating whether or not he should say anything more on the matter. 'I can tell you one thing for nothing, sweetheart,' he said at last. 'The McCraes are very good haters and they don't forget easily. Now I don't know how much Curran's told you about this

Fiona business, but it cut Aunt Margaret as well as Fiona when he broke it off with Fiona.'

Nicola nodded, her eyes downcast. 'Yes, I know, Curran did tell me.'

'And you know that Aunt Margaret holds you to blame for him breaking it off. Though why the hell she should I can't imagine. I gather you didn't even know about Fiona until after you arrived here.'

'I didn't.'

'Well, whichever way it goes, Aunt Margaret's fingered you as the villainess and she'll not let you forget it in a hurry, I can promise you. As I said, the McCraes are good haters and they have long memories.'

Nicola shook her head; her heart felt cold and heavy and she felt horribly vulnerable suddenly as she stood there in the big studio with that picture of Fiona McNee looking at her and smiling. 'I – I find it so hard to believe,' she said at last. 'How can she do things like this? What does she hope to achieve?'

He shrugged, the blue eyes watching her steadily and curiously. 'I guess she thinks she can drive you out in time, make you so uneasy that you leave.' Nicola blinked and he smiled slowly, one brow raised in query. 'Could she do that, Nicky? Would you pack up and go?'

Nicola shook her head, horribly uncertain just how she would react to another surprise like this one. 'I – I don't think so,' she told him slowly. 'I'm pretty obstinate in my own way.'

'I only wish I'd come in here first thing,' he said ruefully. 'I could have clipped her wings like I did last time.'

'Last time?'

He grinned. 'Yes. You remember I had something tucked under my arm when I came down from taking your bags up that first day you arrived?' Nicola nodded, remembering that she had thought she recognized it as a photograph. She remembered too the burst of anger she had overheard from Curran after they had thought her out of earshot.

'It looked like a photograph,' she said, and he nodded.

'It was. Somebody had seen fit to put a photo of Fiona beside your bed. I whisked it away before it did any damage that time – pity I didn't see this painting too.'

Nicola shuddered, hugging herself tightly. 'I – I feel as if I'm – as if I'm being haunted,' she said. She looked round the studio curiously. 'Curran says this studio was made for Fiona too.'

'It was,' he smiled at her reassuringly. 'But she doesn't haunt me, so I shouldn't worry too much about her if I were you. If you let Aunt Margaret see that you've dug in your stubborn little heels she'll give up in time.'

'I hope so.'

'You've come to sit for me again?' He asked the question quietly, and she remembered the incident on the moor yesterday, and coloured.

'If you want me to,' she said, keeping her eyes on the picture propped against the wall.

'I do.' He looked at her for a moment, then lifted her chin with one finger. 'Do you want to go on with it?'

She nodded, evading his hold. 'Of course. It was you who called a halt yesterday.'

For a moment he stood silent, then he laughed suddenly and pointed her in the direction of the window seat. 'Sometimes I don't quite know what you're all about, honey. Now go and sit there like a good girl and let me get to work, O.K.?'

'It's only O.K. if you stop talking to me as if I was a five—'

'I know, I know.' He held up his two hands defensively. 'As if you were a five-year-old. O.K., sweetheart, I'll remember you're a big girl and mind my p's and q's, but have a heart, will you, and try to pretend you're a five-year-old. I have a hunch we'll get along better that way.'

Nicola did a great deal of heart-searching all the time she was sitting still in the studio – whether or not she should tell Curran about the portrait of Fiona that had mysteriously appeared on the easel in Mitchell's studio. She did not for one minute believe that Curran himself had put it there; it would have been against his own interests. Whether he would be prepared to accept the suggestion that his aunt was responsible for the gesture was yet to be seen, but she felt she should let him know what had happened.

Her opportunity came that same evening when they were in the garden and walking along by the sun-warmed wall of the east wing. She chose her moment and plunged in, her heart hammering nervously against her ribs as she told him.

'You – you must be joking,' he said, when she had finished. 'You *must* be joking or imagining things, Nicola, there's no other explanation.'

'I'm doing neither, Curran.' There was a spot of angry colour on each cheek as he looked down at her and his brown eyes were unfamiliarly hard. 'I wouldn't joke about a thing like that,' she told him. 'You must know I wouldn't.'

He brought them to a halt, his hands hard on her shoulders, his mouth tight-lipped. 'You say the painting was on the easel in the studio?'

Nicola nodded. 'Yes. When I went in this morning I saw it. I – I thought at first it was one that Mitch had done, then he came in and said he knew nothing about it, and I believe him, Curran.'

He still frowned and she thought he too knew who had put the portrait of Fiona where she would probably see it. 'What was it like?'

She described the painting, surprised to realize how much detail she could remember. 'Mitch told me it was a picture of Fiona. I wouldn't have known, of course, but the name was on the back of it.'

'He'd probably recognize her anyway,' he said, and Nicola stared at him for a moment.

'He – he knew her?' she asked, and he nodded.

'He met her when he was here before, about ten years ago.'

'Oh – I see.'

'Of course she was only about thirteen or fourteen then, so he may not have done.'

'Not right off he couldn't have done,' Nicola told him, remembering his first remark. 'He thought it was someone I knew.'

His mouth twisted into a caricature of a smile. 'So much for Fiona's hero-worship,' he said, and pulled a face when she looked puzzled. 'She thought he was the last word when he was here last,' he explained. 'Of course he was already in his middle twenties and a very successful business man, so I suppose it was the idea of his image that she admired.'

'You were jealous?' She thought he looked startled at that, and wondered what on earth had prompted the question.

'I suppose I might have been,' he admitted at last. 'I was very young and in the throes of calf-love.'

'Did – did Mitch play up to her?'

He looked at her for a moment as if he suspected something more than mere curiosity behind the question, then he curled his lip. 'Not him,' he told her. 'Anything young and sweet leaves him cold. He likes sophistication and – well, you know the rest.'

For a moment she made no comment, then she looked up at him with a faint smile of reproach. 'Do you count me in that class as well?' she asked.

'Good lord, no!' He stared at her aghast. 'What on

earth made you ask that?'

'The fact that you're always so suspicious about my being with him alone,' she told him. 'You must think he finds me attractive, the fuss you make.'

He hugged her close to him, his face against her hair. 'I'm jealous of anyone that comes near you,' he said. 'You're special.'

'I see.' They seemed to have strayed from their original subject, she thought, though whether he had deliberately led her away from the matter of the portrait or not she was uncertain.

'That picture of Fiona,' she said, determined not to be sidetracked. 'Do you know it, Curran?'

He frowned, confirming her guess that he wanted the subject changed. 'Yes, I know it,' he admitted, reluctantly it was obvious. 'It sounds like the one that usually hangs in Aunt Margaret's room. Alec McNee gave it to her last year when she asked for a memento of Fiona.'

'I see.' She remembered his telling her about Fiona trying to follow in her father's steps as a painter. 'Did he paint it himself?' she asked, and he nodded.

'Yes.' He did not like talking about it, she thought, but she was more than ever curious about Fiona now. 'He often painted her. She was his favourite subject.'

'It's very good.'

'He's a good artist.'

'Did – did you have one of her?'

He looked discomfited for a moment. 'Yes, I have one,' he admitted at last.

Present tense, she noticed, but did not comment on it, only wondering at his still having it in the circumstances. Far more usual to have returned it or have denied having it.

'Curran—' She did not quite know how she was going to word what she had to say, but the urge to say it was irresistible. 'Did – did you love her very much. When you became engaged to her, I mean?'

He was silent for so long that she wondered if he had chosen to ignore the question, then he spoke slowly and as if he chose every word with care, afraid of using the wrong ones. 'I suppose I loved her,' he said. 'I loved her in one way and not in another. I think perhaps I knew her too well to be quite sure how I felt about her.'

'You – you didn't realize how badly hurt she would be when you – when you told her about me?'

'Of course I didn't.' He looked at her then, though it was a hasty look and he lowered his gaze again quickly, one finger tracing the curved neckline of her frock, concentrating on that. 'I had no intention of hurting anybody, you must believe that, Nicola.'

'I do.' She sighed and turned again to continue walking, the gravel crunching under her feet. 'I believe you because I couldn't bear it if I didn't, Curran. I – I can't get her out of my mind lately, and I can't help wishing that I hadn't come here. At least not while your aunt's here and feeling the way she does.'

He caught up with her and took her arm, his fingers tight and digging into her flesh. 'You think it was Aunt

Margaret who put that picture in the studio, don't you?'

'Who else could it have been?'

'You knew it wasn't me?'

She nodded. 'Of course I knew it wasn't you. As far as I know you don't want me to leave Malinbrae, and that seems to be the main reason for these – these hints. Mitch told me about the photograph,' she added.

Curran frowned. 'He didn't have to do that, you need not have known.'

'Curran,' she tried not to sound impatient, 'if I'm to be subjected to a war of nerves I'd sooner know what I'm up against. I don't like not knowing where I stand.'

'I suppose I should have told you,' he admitted reluctantly.

'You should have told me about Fiona, and you should have warned me about how your aunt felt. It would have been much fairer to me.'

'I know.' He halted her again and turned her to face him, his good-looking face anxious and even more boyish in the gathering dusk. 'Darling, you won't leave, will you? You won't let Aunt Margaret drive you away?'

It was some seconds before she answered, then she smiled and shook her head. 'I won't,' she said. 'I don't like being *driven* to anything.'

'And will you believe how sorry I am that I didn't tell you about – about all this before you came here?'

'I believe you.'

He drew her close in his arms and kissed her. His arms strong and comforting, but still in Nicola's mind was the idea that once he had felt this way about Fiona, had held her in his arms and declared his love for her. Fiona had believed him and been let down badly – how much better could she herself expect to fare?

CHAPTER SEVEN

NICOLA had no idea what happened when Mitchell returned the portrait of Fiona to its owner, for he had said nothing about it, but whatever it was it had done nothing to improve her relations with the older woman, and she could not help but regret it. Not that Miss McCrae had said anything either, but from the way she often regarded her, Nicola knew that Mitchell must have returned her property. What still puzzled her was whether Curran had mentioned it to his aunt or not.

If his manner when she had told him was anything to judge by he would almost surely have given his aunt an opinion and, much as she knew the older woman disliked her, she felt more pity than anything else for her. She would like to have offered a truce, but that stern, forbidding face discouraged any such move.

It was because Curran was obliged to leave her to her own devices one afternoon that Nicola decided to ride alone, the first time she had done so since her fall. He was now almost annoyingly anxious about her and insisted on always being with her when she rode, which somewhat restricted her movements. Ian McCrae was as usual also busy, and she felt she could not face the prospect of Margaret McCrae's company alone, so she had said nothing to Curran about her decision, but simply made up her mind to go.

The weather the past few weeks, since Nicola had been at Malinbrae, had been beautiful, and it still held, although it now showed early signs of autumn as the days moved into September. The mists in the glen clung that little bit longer in the mornings and the sun was less hot and more mellowly warm.

Having spent the morning in the studio with Mitchell, she was glad to be out in the air, and the thought of a solitary ride appealed to her. She had been allowed a brief peep at the part-finished portrait this morning, although it was obvious that Mitchell was more than a little reluctant to let her see it.

Judging it on as much as was completed, she had been surprised at the quality of the work. Even allowing for the fact that Curran would never have given his cousin credit for anything without very good reason, she had been very surprised how good the painting was. When she said as much to the artist, however, he had laughed and said he was flattered, and that he supposed she would have been better pleased if it had been less commendable.

She had refused to be drawn into one of their interminable arguments, however, and she had stuck out her chin and maintained a dignified silence, a gesture that had given him further cause for amusement. If she was honest about how she felt, having seen the painting, she was much more excited than she cared to admit.

She walked across the stable yard, neat and trim in

cream-coloured trousers and a blue shirt, so pre-occupied that she started nervously when someone spoke from the dim interior of the stable.

'Hi there!'

She peered into the shadows, although she had no need to identify the speaker. 'Hello, Mitch.'

He came out into the sun, leading the big grey he invariably rode, eyeing her quizzically. 'You don't sound very pleased to see me,' he accused.

In truth Nicola was unsure whether she was pleased to see him or not. Certainly when he had first spoken she had hoped that he was just coming back from a ride and not just starting out, or he would probably suggest coming with her, and she could never quite disguise the fact that she was still vaguely uneasy whenever she was alone with him.

It was bad enough when they were in the studio, but out there on the vast endlessness of the moor, she must always be reminded of that disquieting moment when he had kissed her – a kiss he swore she had provoked, and which her own response to had both surprised and disturbed her.

'I don't see how you can tell *how* I feel from just a couple of words,' she told him, and he laughed.

'With you it's easy, honey,' he said. 'You're not difficult to read.'

'So you tell me.'

'Well, it's true,' he insisted, smiling down at her. 'For one thing those big grey eyes of yours always give you away, and you frowned too.' He mocked her own small expression with a thunderously black scowl. 'You know the kind of frown – oh lord, I hope he's not going to ask to come with me. Am I right?'

'You're right,' she agreed maliciously, but could not resist a smile, and he laughed again.

'There you are, you see,' he told her. 'What I don't guess you tell me.'

'Ooh! Why do you always have to score off me?'

He stood for a moment, one thumb hooked into the front pocket of the inevitable jeans, one brow raised in query. 'I didn't know I did,' he said, as if he had given it some thought. 'And I don't think I do, honey. You're just too touchy.'

'Oh yes, that's something else you're always saying,' Nicola informed him. 'And I don't think I *am* touchy, as you call it.'

'You are too!' He was laughing at her, but his face was set into mock solemnity. 'Why, you rise every time I say anything to you.'

'Only because you mean me to,' Nicola retorted.

The blue eyes gleamed wickedly at her and she knew that if she looked at him for very much longer she too would have to laugh. There was something infectious about his amusement even though it was directed at her. 'Maybe I do at that,' he admitted, and she stuck out her chin at him.

'There you are, you see,' she said triumphantly. 'It's *you* who starts it every time, and then you tell me I'm touchy when I answer back.'

'Aah! Poor little injured innocent!' One hand

stroked her cheek gently and she hastily moved back out of reach, her pulse skipping wildly.

'Don't, Mitch!'

He looked almost startled for a moment, then turned and walked back into the stable, calling over his shoulder as he went, 'O.K., honey, don't bite. Are you taking the roan?'

She hesitated, wondering whether it would be better to change her mind about going after all. 'I – I don't know.'

He reappeared round the edge of the roan's stall, looking curious. 'What's that supposed to mean?'

'I – I mean I'm not at all sure that I want to go out after all. Curran doesn't like me riding alone, since I was thrown.'

It was, she realized, a second too late, more or less an invitation for him to join her. 'You won't be alone if you're with me,' he told her, and grinned. 'What you really meant was that you don't know whether to change your mind because I'm going out too, isn't that it?'

'Not necessarily,' she denied uneasily. 'It's just that—'

'Well, you don't have to worry, honey,' he assured her before she could finish. 'I've told you before, you're safe enough with me.'

'And you've proved I'm not!' The retort was impulsive and unthinking and he stood there for a breathless second, that exciting, indefinable challenge sending her pulses skipping out of control, then he came towards her again as she stood in the doorway to the stable.

He rested one hand on the frame of the door above her head and leaned close enough for her to feel the warmth of him, although she pressed herself as hard as she could back against the unyielding wood. 'I begin to think you're a witch,' he informed her, soft-voiced, his eyes searching her face and coming to rest on her mouth. 'Although I'm not sure I shouldn't spell it with a "b". If you do this to Curran I wonder you haven't driven the poor guy out of his mind by now.'

'I don't—'

'Do you really know what temptation you put in my way?' he went on relentlessly. 'You'd be enough to try the resistance of a saint, and God knows, I'm no saint.'

'But I don't—' Nicola tried again, and got no further this time.

'Now don't say you don't *try* to raise my temperature,' he told her. 'I just won't believe it.'

'I don't try to do anything,' she protested, wondering if she was speaking the truth, or at least all of it. She did find him attractive, most women would, but she never consciously tried to be provocative, although he accused her of it.

The blue eyes studied her for a moment longer, then he rubbed a hand on the back of his head and sighed deeply. 'I guess you don't at that,' he allowed. 'It's just natural chemistry, and in somebody as young and — O.K., O.K.' He held up his hands when he recognized the beginnings of a protest, moving away from her to lean against the opposite side of the doorway, studying her for a while with a smile she found discomfiting. 'O.K., honey,' he said at last quietly, 'are you going to ride that roan or not?'

'I think I might,' she said, as quietly as he. 'Just a little way.'

'Good.' He smiled as if the answer satisfied him, and disappeared into the stable again to fetch the mount.

He helped her to mount, then sat on the big grey looking at her with one brow cocked quizzically. 'Am I to be allowed to ride with you?' he asked. 'Or am I still not to be trusted?'

Nicola held the rein tightly in her hands and put her heels to the roan, calling back over her shoulder to him as she went, 'You can come or stay, I don't care.'

She heard the deep sound of his laughter and a few seconds later the grey thundered alongside her own mount, strong brown hands holding his speed down to that of the slower animal.

'Have you decided where we're going?' he asked, and she shook her head.

'No.'

'What about the Glen of Sighs?' he suggested, and Nicola turned and looked at him curiously.

'The Glen of Sighs?'

'Don't tell me you haven't been there.'

'I haven't,' she admitted. 'I've never even heard of it.'

'You have now,' he told her, and cocked a curious

brow at her again. 'Hasn't Curran taken you?'

'No.'

'Then how about breaking new ground?'

He could undoubtedly be very persuasive, and she suspected he was prepared to be and she hesitated only because she felt oddly uneasy about accepting the invitation. 'Is – is it very far?'

'Not as the horse gallops,' he informed her facetiously. 'It'll take us about half an hour, a little longer I guess if we adjust our pace to Brownie's.'

It was further afield than she had intended going and she wondered what he would say if she decided against it. No doubt he would make some comment designed to draw her into yet another argument.

'Maybe,' she agreed cautiously.

'Are you playing that yes or maybe game again?' he demanded.

'I'm just trying to make up my mind,' she told him shortly. 'I hadn't planned on going that far this afternoon, and I won't be browbeaten into making rash decisions.'

'Rash decisions?' He looked at her down the length of his arrogant nose. 'For crying out loud, Nicky, we're only going for a ride, I'm not kidnapping you.'

'Oh, all right!'

She could feel the colour in her cheeks and knew he was as much amused as impatient at her hesitation, and she felt she could not face either at the moment, so she put her heels to Brownie again and went on ahead of him, her back stiff and resentful.

He made no move for several seconds, then he came alongside again. 'O.K., come on if you're coming,' he said then, and spurred the grey into a gallop that the roan had no hope of matching. 'Come on!' he called over one shoulder.

She responded instantly, sending the roan after them, although there was no hope of catching them. The roan responded gallantly and kicked up his heels in fine style as he pursued his stablemate, flying over the turf and heather like the wind.

The warm wind flicked Nicola's tawny hair back from her face and brought bright colour to her cheeks as she urged him on to greater efforts, the thrill of the chase and a wild sense of exhilaration stirring her blood and bringing a smile to her face as she bent low along the horse's neck.

Down the wide glen they went to the very edge of the little loch, glinting in the sun, and there Mitchell reined in the grey so suddenly that he sat back on his haunches, his head back and anxious to be away again. It was a gesture of either skill or bravado, perhaps both; certainly there was a hint of challenge in the smile he turned on her when she joined him.

She brought Brownie to a halt in less spectacular fashion and sat for a moment conscious of the deep silence around them, and the overawing vastness of the moor.

'You'll never make a racehorse out of him,' he told her, and Nicola patted the roan's silky neck affectionately, her mouth reproachful.

'He did very well,' she said. 'We've no desire to compete with Nijinsky, have we, Brownie?'

'Loyalty!' he jeered softly, his eyes gleaming with some expression she could not quite interpret. 'You like that old haybag, don't you?'

'I do,' Nicola declared staunchly, 'and I wish you wouldn't call him names, it's – it's unkind.'

He burst into laughter at that, and turned the grey round once more, to walk around the rim of the loch. 'Oh well, from now on we can take things a bit easier, now I've taken some of the energy out of Cloud.'

They rode easily, and spoke little, both of them seemingly affected by the peace and tranquillity of the country, and content to just take things easy for the time being. It was warm in the sun and Nicola lifted her face to the soft wind that wisped her hair about her face and neck, unconscious of the way he watched her until he spoke.

'O.K.?' The question was asked softly and she merely nodded in reply, responding to the slow smile instinctively.

They were heading in the direction of the hills that Nicola had decided to visit once before and been discouraged by the seeming distance of them. On past the place where Brownie had unseated her, and the wildcat had sent him flying for home without her. There were more trees here, rustling quietly in the late summer wind and softening the expanse of the moor with contours of green.

'Nearly there.' She glanced up at him, startled out of

a reverie, and he smiled. 'How're you doing?'

'Fine, thank you.' She felt a sudden strange shyness again and wished he had not broken the silence.

He led the way down a slight incline and round another swathe of trees, then turned to see her reaction to the sudden sight of a small, shallow glen with a tiny church in the hollow of its hand, and one or two small stone cottages in a jumble of habitation around it.

'Oh, Mitch, it's lovely!' The exclamation was impulsive, and she looked at the collection of buildings almost as if she expected them to disappear at any minute. 'It's – it's like Brigadoon!'

'So it is,' he agreed, and smiled at her fancy. 'Though I hadn't thought of it till now.'

'Is this the Glen of Sighs?'

He nodded. 'That's right.'

'Oh, but it doesn't *look* sad. Well, I feel it should,' she added hastily and defensively when he smiled. 'With a name like Glen of Sighs it should have a – a sadness about it. Is there a story behind the name?'

'Of course,' he agreed. 'Though I'm no expert on Scottish legend, you'll have to ask Ian about that, or Curran. I was told it when I was here before, but I don't remember it well enough to tell it without spoiling its point.'

She remembered that Curran had told her he had spent time at Malinbrae before. 'Oh yes,' she said. 'You've been here before, haven't you?'

'I have, about ten years ago.' He looked at her curiously. 'Did Curran tell you that?'

She nodded. 'When I told him you said it was Fiona in that painting. He said you'd probably recognized her, but you didn't, did you?'

'She'd changed,' he said. 'She was only a schoolgirl when I saw her.'

'And she had a crush on you,' she said softly.

He smiled wryly. 'I tried not to notice,' he told her. 'It seemed the kindest thing to do in the circumstances.'

She glanced at him through her lashes. 'You'd take it all in your stride, I suppose,' she guessed. 'Being swooned over by young girls is probably all in a day's work to you.'

He raised surprised brows at that, and she wondered if he would resent it, but he was still smiling. 'You flatter me,' he told her. 'I've told you before, honey, I don't play with little girls.'

'I remember, but *you* were ten years younger then, as well.'

'But I still wasn't interested in schoolgirls, Nicky.'

'Curran was jealous,' she said quietly, and he raised a brow.

'He told you that too? He *was* forthcoming, wasn't he?'

'Only because I asked him,' she admitted. 'He didn't really want to mention her at all.'

'No, I guess he wouldn't at that.'

'Mitch—' She bit on her lip, hesitating. 'You – you weren't here when – when Curran broke it off with Fiona, were you?'

He shook his head. 'No, I wasn't.' He looked across at her, his blue eyes steady. 'Did you think I was?'

'No.' She followed his meaning then and shook her head hastily. 'Oh no, of course not! I know you had nothing to do with – with what happened, but—' she eased her shoulders in a hopeless sort of shrug – 'I – I just wondered what really *did* happen, that's all.'

He was silent for a while, then he reached out a hand and covered hers for a brief moment. 'She worries you, doesn't she, honey?' he guessed softly.

'A – a little,' she confessed, and wished there was something she could do about the wild beat of her heart.

'Don't let it,' he said. 'She was a nice girl as I remember her, Nicky. A whole lot nicer than the people who're trying to keep her alive to haunt you.'

'I didn't know about her, I honestly didn't.'

'I know you didn't.'

She was silent for a moment, then she eased back her shoulders as if determinedly shifting the weight that had settled there. 'It must be the Glen of Sighs,' she told him. 'I've been affected by its reputation, and it's much too pretty a place to make me feel miserable about anything.'

'Maybe I shouldn't have brought you,' he suggested, but she would have none of that, and smiled at him.

'I'm glad of the chance to see it,' she told him. 'I can't think why Curran hasn't brought me here to see it.'

They rode right on through the little collection of

stone houses, stopping briefly to admire the tiny church, then on through the other side into the open country again. There was one small house on its own beside a burn that fed a much bigger river further up the glen, and they rode as far as the swift-flowing water to let the horses snuffle its coolness.

'Can *we* drink that water, do you think?' Nicola asked, and Mitchell pulled a face.

'I don't think I'd care to, not after the horses have been in it,' he told her. 'But I could ask the householder for some water if you're really dying of thirst.'

'I'm not exactly dying,' she admitted, 'but I am thirsty.'

'Your wish is my command.' He dismounted and walked over to the cottage, while Nicola got down, looking around her curiously, and thinking how wonderful it would be to live in a place as beautiful and peaceful as this.

'Nicky!' He was calling her over and she led the roan across to the cottage and joined him at the door.'Would you rather have a cup of tea?'

A round, friendly face appeared at the doorway behind him and Nicola smiled at the owner of it. 'I'd *love* a cup of tea,' she said. 'Thank you very much.'

'Come away in.' The voice had the soft lilt of the Highlands and the woman signed to them to come inside and sit down. The inside of the cottage was small but incredibly neat and clean, and the walls white-painted stone, covered with cut-out pictures and old photographs. It was a homely place and Nicola felt immediately at ease, settling into an old wooden arm-chair comfortably.

The tea was already brewed and much stronger than Nicola liked as a rule, but it was very welcome. 'Ye'll be visitors ta Scotland?' their hostess guessed in her gentle voice. 'Ye're no from these parts, I know, for I know every soul this ten miles round.'

'That's right,' Mitchell agreed, after having taken a cautious sip of the tea. 'We're foreigners, I guess you'd say.'

'American,' the woman said with a smile. 'It's no hard ta spot the accent.'

'Only me,' Mitchell corrected her. 'I guess Nicky wouldn't thank you for calling her an American.'

Nicola acknowledged the fact with a wry face that wrinkled her nose, and their hostess smiled knowingly. 'Och aye,' she said softly, 'but the lassie's ready ta accept it for the sake o' true love, eh?'

Nicola almost choked over her tea, but Mitchell seemed to be finding the whole thing highly amusing, and he nodded, his eyes gleaming wickedly at Nicola. 'I guess so,' he agreed.

'But—' Nicola began, then stopped, her eyes picking out one particular picture among the galaxy on the wall beside her. The pretty oval face with its crown of dark hair, and soft gentle expression was familiar. Uncomfortably and disturbingly familiar.

'Ye're looking at ma bairns,' the woman said, catching her interest, but missing her breathless reaction to the sight of Fiona McNee among her collection. 'I was midwife hereabouts for more than thirty years,' she explained, obviously proud of her record. 'An' many's the time I've brought a bairn inta the world and *their* bairns after that. Everyone hereabouts comes inta the world wi' Agnes McKie's assistance.'

'It's quite a record,' Mitchell told her, unaware of Nicola's discovery.

'Aye, I'm quite proud o' masel',' the old lady told him, and moved to stand beside Nicola. The picture that had caught her eye was touched gently with a gnarled forefinger and the woman sighed. 'Sometimes it's no always happy things I'm called on ta do,' she added softly. 'Yon pretty wee creature now. Everything ta live for, ye'd think. A braw man ta marry her, and then—' She used her hands expressively and Nicola felt her own hands tighten into balls as she clutched the tea-cup.

Her voice had a husky sound when she spoke and she knew that at last Mitchell had realized there was something wrong when he looked at her sharply, his eyes narrowed. 'What happened to her?' she asked.

'Och, she couldna take the shock o' being let down so badly, poor wee lamb.' The soft, elderly voice was lost in reminiscence. 'She drove her car off the road and killed hersel', poor silly wee creature.'

'Oh no!'

'I laid her out,' the old woman went on, and it was doubtful if she had even heard the interjection. 'It was kept quiet, o' course, for the father's sake as well as the wee girl, but I knew from him, the poor man, he was near mad wi' grief.'

Nicola could feel her knees weak and shaking as she got to her feet and Mitchell reached out and touched her arm gently. 'We'd better be going, honey,' he told her softly, and she nodded without speaking. He turned to the old woman, who shook herself out of her reverie with an apologetic smile.

'I'm sorry I rambled on at ye,' she told him. 'I don't see sa many folk ta talk to an' I've sa many things ta talk about.'

'It's been very interesting, Mrs. McKie,' he told her, his voice gentle and understanding, as it was for Nicola. 'And thank you for the tea.'

'Och, ye're more than welcome ta come again any time,' she assured him as she saw them to the door. 'Haste ye back.'

The old words of parting saw them on their way, and Nicola wondered how she managed to smile as she turned to wave goodbye. Mitchell said nothing for a while, then he turned and looked at her steadily.

'That picture of Fiona,' he said quietly. 'Don't let it get you, Nicky.'

'How can I help it?' Nicola asked despairingly, her hands clenched over the rein. 'You heard what she said about – about how she died.'

'I heard what she said,' he agreed, 'but she's an old woman, Nicky, and she's saying what she thinks, not what she knows for certain. Even if it is true, and I'm not prepared to admit it is, how does it make *you* in any way to blame?'

'I – I don't know.' She felt tears burning behind her eyes and shook her head. 'I'm – I'm just being silly, I suppose.'

'You're just being illogical and feminine,' he told her with a wry smile.

'I can't help it.'

'I know, but you must try. I know it sounds hard and you probably think I'm a callous, unfeeling brute, but she's gone, honey, and there's nothing you or I or anyone else can do about it.'

'I'm sorry.'

'That's the whole point, you don't have to be sorry, you have nothing to be sorry about.'

'No, no, I suppose not.' She looked at him, her eyes still seeking reassurance, dark and troubled. 'I'm sorry, Mitch.'

'And for Pete's sake don't start that I'm sorry line again,' he warned her with mock severity, 'or I'll tan your beautiful hide. O.K.?'

'I'm—' She caught his eye and smiled a little uncertainly. 'I nearly did it again, didn't I?'

'You did.' He leaned over and covered her hands with one of his. 'Forget about Fiona, Nicky, it's the only way.'

'I'll try.'

'Good girl!' He squeezed her fingers and urged the grey to a faster pace. 'Come on, let's move a little faster, huh?'

They were even quieter on the way back than they had been before, and Nicola knew things could never be quite the same again. No matter how Mitchell urged her to forget about Fiona she could never get the girl out of her mind. Always, whatever she did, wherever she went there was something to remind her of the girl she had replaced in Curran's affections, and now this last, most disturbing revelation of all.

'Can you face an inquisition?' Mitchell asked softly, breaking into her thoughts, and she looked at him startled for a moment. He nodded his head in the direction of the loch they had just left behind and she saw another rider approaching. 'Curran,' he said briefly.

'Oh no!'

She had a brief glimpse of a slightly surprised look on Mitchell's face, then she put her heels to the roan and sent him into a gallop. 'Come on, Brownie!' she cried, and set off across the glen too fast for Curran ever to hope to catch her.

The speed they were going whipped back her hair and coloured her cheeks and she did not stop to think what emotion had urged her to escape from Curran's inevitable anger at seeing her with Mitchell. She could not face it at the moment, and she did not care what construction he put on her sudden and impulsive escape.

She had gone only a few yards when the grey came charging up beside them, and Mitchell's lean brown face grinned at her knowingly, his voice thinned by the wind they were creating. 'You've done it now,' he told her, and seemed quite unconcerned about it.

She did not reply, but let Brownie have his head for

the rest of the way home, bringing him to a halt, blowing hard and steaming, in the stable yard. She swung down from the saddle without waiting for assistance and Mitchell came and took the reins from her.

'Feeling better?' he asked.

Nicola shook her head. 'No,' she said, her voice small and tight in her throat. 'I wish I hadn't done it. He'll only think the worst.'

'The worst being that we were—' He used a dark brow to emphasize his meaning.

'I just couldn't face a scene,' she told him. 'I had no other reason.'

'Of course you hadn't.'

'Anyway,' she glanced at him through her lashes, 'I don't really see that Curran can say very much about it. He told me himself that you weren't interested in anything young and sweet, which is what he considers me.'

'And he's right.'

She looked up at him, his blue eyes dark with some expression she could not definitely define, and that hint of challenge in the way he was standing, the two horses held tightly by the reins in one strong hand. Her breath caught in her throat and she could feel the wild hammering of her heart as she sought to sound cool and controlled as she turned her back.

'Thank you for helping me, Mitch.'

'Helping you?'

She turned again and smiled faintly at him. 'You've tried to help me lay the ghost of Fiona,' she reminded him. 'I don't know how well you've succeeded, but I'm grateful that you tried.'

She never knew what impulse prompted her to tip-toe and brush her lips softly against his, but he let go the horses and swept her against him suddenly, his arm and his mouth hard and somehow desperate, while Fiona receded rapidly to the back of her mind.

CHAPTER EIGHT

CURRAN had never looked so angry in all the time she had known him, and Nicola thought she had not even realized he was capable of such anger. He did not even look like the same man. His good-looking, boyish face was set hard and there was a stony look about the brown eyes whenever he looked at her.

She had contrived to avoid being alone with him last night. Dinner had been in company with Ian and Margaret McCrae, as usual, and after dinner she had managed to inveigle Curran's father to show her how to play Canasta. She knew Curran was waiting his chance to catch her alone, but she was not prepared to face him alone at the moment. He was fuming with righteous indignation at seeing her in what she was bound to admit had been a very compromising position with his cousin, and she was not at all sure just how she was going to explain it.

She had not been quite fair, she supposed, in so hurriedly leaving when she saw him coming across the moor, but her mind had been in such a turmoil after hearing old Mrs. McKie's version of how Fiona died, that she had not stopped to consider his feelings at all.

Miss McCrae had left no doubt that she thought Fiona had deliberately crashed her car, although

Curran had denied it. Ian McCrae had been less adamant either way, but now this latest opinion had come, entirely unsolicited, from someone outside the close circle of Fiona's family and friends.

It would be little use, she thought ruefully, trying to avoid Curran this morning, for almost certainly he would be in the dining-room having breakfast when she went down, as he always was. She bathed and dressed, perhaps a little more tardily than was usual, and went downstairs.

The big dining-room looked bright and cheerful as always, but its sole occupant got to his feet when she came in with a frown black enough to darken the brightest day. She hesitated when she saw him, and steeled herself for the inevitable disapproval, but nevertheless gave him a brief, wary smile which he chose to ignore.

'Sit down, Nicola, I want to talk to you.' He sounded so cold and impersonal that she almost obeyed instinctively, but instead remained on her feet and tried not to look guilty.

'I'd rather stay on my feet,' she told him. 'If you're going to tell me off about something, and it looks as if you are, then I'd rather hear it standing up.'

He looked at her narrowly, his fingers rapping a restless tattoo on the edge of the table. 'You deliberately avoided me last night,' he accused, and she nodded, looking at those tapping fingers as if they fascinated her.

'I admit it,' she allowed, readily enough. 'I didn't

147

want to quarrel with you.'

'But you're ready to this morning?'

She raised her eyes and looked at him steadily. 'Not unless you make me,' she told him. 'You seem bent on quarrelling with me, but it isn't my idea at all.'

'Good grief!' He ran his hands through his hair and looked at her exasperatedly. 'Didn't you expect me to be angry?'

'Yes, of course I did,' Nicola told him. 'That's why I avoided you. I hoped you would have – cooled down a bit by this morning.'

He stared at her for a moment as if he could not understand her at all. 'Cooled down? You expect me to cool down after what I saw yesterday?' He shook his head slowly, as if it was all too much for him to comprehend. 'I come back in time to see my fiancée in – with another man, kissing him, and you expect me to cool down overnight?'

The possessiveness of the 'fiancée' startled her and she shook her head. 'I'm not your fiancée, Curran.'

'You are as far as I'm concerned,' he told her shortly, and Nicola flushed, lifting her chin, ready to argue the point.

'Well, you're wrong,' she informed him. 'You know you are, Curran. I've never agreed to marry you.'

'I don't care whether you've actually said you will or not,' he insisted stubbornly. 'That's the reason you're here, to meet my family and do all the usual things that people do before they get married.'

That much was, she supposed, true enough to defy

argument, and she sighed. 'I'm sorry if you think I've behaved badly,' she said.

'You were kissing him.' He seemed determined to see the argument through, and she knew she would come out of it as the losing side. 'In the circumstances I think I have a right to be angry whether you agree that you're my fiancée or not.'

She turned away from him, the memory of Fiona stirring again. If only he would not insist on referring to her as his fiancée; it always reminded her that Fiona *had* been engaged to him, and she did not at all like the idea of being in the dead girl's shoes.

'If it upset you, I'm sorry,' she said quietly. 'I – I know how you feel, Curran, and I know you don't like Mitch, but—'

'I *love* you,' he insisted. 'You know how much I love you, Nicola, how can you let him – manhandle you like that?'

'He kissed me,' Nicola declared shortly, her cheeks flushed. 'That's all, Curran, and you have no call to make it sound like anything worse.'

'I just don't understand you.' For the moment he looked much more like his familiar self again with a puzzled look in his eyes and a deep crease between his brows.

'No, I don't think you do,' she said regretfully. 'I had no intention of hurting you, Curran, please believe me. I was – I was just grateful to Mitch, that's all.'

'Grateful?'

She nodded, seeing a full explanation as inevitable

now. 'We went riding together,' she began, and saw his frown deepen.

'You know I don't like you going without me,' he said.

'I know you don't, but what you *don't* realize is that your aunt isn't very good company for me when you and your father are out. I – I just couldn't face being alone with her, so I went out. I felt like riding alone and I didn't see why I shouldn't.'

'Alone?' He raised a doubtful brow.

'I went down to the stable to get Brownie and Mitch was there,' she explained. 'He was going out too, so we went together. He suggested we went to the Glen of Sighs and, as I'd never seen it, I thought it was a good idea.'

'I see.' His mouth had a close, tight look again. 'I can guess why he took you there.'

'Can you?' She looked genuinely puzzled and he looked at her uncertainly for a moment.

'Did you stop at the kirk?'

'We stopped and looked at it for a couple of minutes,' she agreed. 'We didn't leave the horses.'

'Didn't you see Fiona's grave?'

Nicola stared at him. 'No,' she said quietly. 'We didn't.'

He looked a little discomfited, as if his suspicions of Mitchell had been dismissed. 'I see.'

'I – I didn't realize she was – she was there.'

'It was her favourite spot,' he said. 'She always loved that little kirk, we were—' He stopped then and his eyes

150

darkened when she looked at him. It was so easy to finish that sentence for him, but she resisted it.

'I didn't know.' She raised her eyes and held his gaze steadily. 'I'm certain Mitch didn't either, Curran. He didn't mention it once.'

'No, maybe not.'

She turned from him again and walked across to the window, looking out at the promise of another sunny day. 'I – I was thirsty and an old woman in the cottage by the stream gave us a cup of tea.'

His silence told its own story, and it was several minutes before he spoke. 'Agnes McKie,' he said then, and there was such a note of resignation in his voice that it drew her pity.

'She – she told us about Fiona,' Nicola said quietly.

'Did she know who you were?'

'No. I saw a picture of Fiona on the wall among that huge collection she has there.'

'She was very fond of Fiona.'

She turned her head and looked at him. 'Curran, did you know that she – she shares your aunt's idea of why Fiona died?'

His eyes had a haunted look and she had never felt more sorry for anyone in her life. If she herself was haunted by Fiona how much more vulnerable was Curran? He had loved her, promised to marry her in that little kirk. Sometimes the thought of her death must be almost too much for him to bear when he thought of his own part in it.

'She told you *her* version, Nicola,' he told her, his voice harsh and unsteady. 'Alec McNee's version, Aunt Margaret's version.'

'Three people with one idea, Curran.'

'No, no!' He turned her to face him, his hands gripping her cruelly hard as he forced her to look at him. 'I refuse to believe it! Don't you see, darling? Alec McNee put that idea into the old woman's head, and into Aunt Margaret's too. No one else believes it, because it simply isn't true.'

'Did you know her well enough to be sure of that?'

He blinked at her for a moment, then he shook his head, closing his eyes on the truth he had so far refused to face. 'No – no, I don't believe I did really know her. I knew her all her life, but how can you know what a person will do in – in a moment of despair?'

'Oh, Curran!'

'All right, all right!' He raised his hands to cover his ears. 'I know I should have been more careful how I told Fiona, I should have come home and seen her, told her about you – about how I felt about you, but I was a coward, I suppose. I wrote her a letter instead.'

'And she died.'

He gripped her arms again, his face stonily stubborn, his eyes glittering. 'It wasn't my fault, Nicola, I refuse to believe it was my fault.'

'We'll never really know,' Nicola sighed. 'Only Fiona knew the truth of it, and she can't tell us now.'

It was a relief to spend the morning with Mitchell

again, for at least he was less intense and quarrelsome than Curran, and she went through to the east wing with no qualms at all despite Miss McCrae's knowing eyes following her when she left the room.

The studio was deserted when she went in and she spent a few moments looking at the part finished portrait on the easel, dropping the cover over it hastily when she heard footsteps in the corridor behind her. She turned and smiled a greeting at Mitchell, her hands behind her back, and he looked from her to the easel and back again with one brow lifted expressively.

'You've been looking,' he accused, and came across to her, towering over her like a schoolmaster, a black frown on his face.

'No, I—'

'Don't lie about it and make it worse,' he told her sternly. 'You've looked at it again, and you have no right to take sly peeks until I say you can.'

'I'm sorry.'

'And don't start being sorry again.'

'I – oh, stop being such a grouch!' she told him, walking off with her chin in the air. 'I've had enough of temperament this morning.'

'Curran?' He sounded as if he was uncertain whether to laugh or not, and she turned and looked at him again.

'He was furious, Mitch.'

'About me kissing you?' He sounded so matter-of-fact she wondered at anyone making so much fuss about the incident.

'Oh, I know it doesn't mean a thing to you,' she told him, 'but Curran's very easily hurt by what he considers slights, and I was really on the carpet this morning when I came down to breakfast.'

'Poor little beggar! Did he give you hell, honey?'

'You wouldn't care what he did, would you?' she asked, her chin high, and he laughed.

'Well, you weren't exactly the injured innocent, were you?' he asked. 'In fact you started it, if I remember correctly.'

Nicola stared at him wide-eyed, a picture of righteous indignation. 'Oh, you *mon*ster! If you were a gentleman you'd take the blame and apologize.'

He perched himself on the edge of a high stool he sometimes used, one elbow propped on a knee, the blue eyes narrowed quizzically. 'But you know I'm not a gentleman, honey. I'm an uncouth Yank, remember? What was the rest of it? Brash, uncouth and lacking in polish and breeding, wasn't that it?'

'You've got a long memory,' Nicola retorted, her cheeks pink when she remembered her initial summary of him. 'I bet you even remember the Boston tea-party.'

'Of course – I'm a New Englander.'

'I – I wish you'd forget it, Mitch.' She did not look at him, but down at her hands that folded her skirt into a hundred tiny pleats with unsteady fingers. 'I wish you'd let me forget it too, and start again.'

'You mean you've read that book I gave you and

you now think we might have a veneer of civilization?'

'I mean – I – I might have misjudged you, and if I did I'm sorry.'

'*If* you did?' He laughed softly, and picked up his brushes. 'You're a real cautious little gal, aren't you?'

She said no more for the moment, but went and sat on the window seat, looking out at the sunny garden and noticing that there was still a trace of mist around the hollow places on the moor. On a clear day you could probably see almost as far as the Glen of Sighs, she thought, and hastily recalled her mind. She would think no more about Fiona today.

'A penny for them,' he offered as he studied her carefully before putting paint to canvas, and Nicola turned rather startled eyes on him, then she laughed.

'As a matter of fact,' she told him untruthfully, 'I was wondering about you.'

A brow shot upwards and she thought he had a slightly wary look about him which she had not noticed before. 'Me? What about me?'

'I don't know much about you.'

He laughed, still concentrating on what he was doing. 'Do you have to know about me?' he asked.

'I'm just curious.'

'I'll bet you are,' he chuckled. 'Most females are.'

'I know you're Curran's cousin,' she said, refusing to be deterred. 'And I know your father is brother to

Curran's mother. I know you're a business man, *when* you're working, and I know you're – you're rich.'

'Am I?'

'So Curran said.'

'And what else did Curran say? That I was a pain in the neck to him, and he'd like to see me shipped back home?'

'I can't think *why* he doesn't like you,' she admitted, and for a moment could not understand why he laughed.

'I was under the impression you hated the sight of me,' he told her with a wicked grin. 'You once in-formed me, if my memory serves me correctly, that I was the most hateful man you'd ever met.'

'Oh, there you go again!' Nicola declared crossly. 'Bringing up ancient history.'

'Do I take it you've come across someone even more hateful?' he inquired solemnly. 'Or have you had second thoughts about me?'

She looked out at the garden again, and tried to ignore the way her heart was rapping nervously at her ribs. 'I suppose,' she ventured at last, 'you'll do some-thing drastic if I say I'm sorry?'

He looked up and smiled, that slow, warm smile that took her breath away. 'Not this time, sweetheart,' he said softly.

She turned away hastily lest he should sense how she felt, her hands tight little balls on her lap. 'Then I'm sorry.'

'What else did Cousin Curran tell you?' he asked, his

attention on his work again.

'He said – that you like—'

'He said I like playing around,' he finished for her, his smile still in place. 'And he's right, of course. I like beautiful women, always have, I guess I always will.'

'You've – you've never been married?'

She half expected him to take offence at the extremely personal question, but he seemed unperturbed by it. 'Nope! I've had many a near miss, mind you, but so far I've managed to avoid the noose.' He looked up at her then and she thought he was more serious than he had been so far. 'You may not believe this,' he said quietly and with a slight crook to his mouth, 'but I don't believe in divorce. Now isn't *that* a disgrace for a Yank to admit? Knowing our reputation with you Limeys.'

'I don't think our reputation is much better these days, is it?' she asked, wondering if he was as serious as he had sounded.

'That's why I'm over here for a spell,' he went on as if she had not spoken. 'In my full fighting form I can hold 'em off, but a man not up to his usual form can get roped in to marry some sweet woman who soothes his brow while he's sick, and I didn't want to have any regrets afterwards.'

'Curran said you'd been ill.'

'Not exactly ill,' he corrected her with a wry smile. 'I crashed my car at about eighty miles an hour and I got a bit bent in the process.'

'Oh dear!'

'Oh, I'm O.K. now,' he assured her with a smile for her concern. 'It was six months ago and I took a little time getting over it, but this couple of months here have put me on my feet again.'

'Does – does that mean you'll be going back?'

He did not look up this time but kept his eyes on his work. 'Quite soon now. I have a lot of catching up to do and Pop will think I've left the firm if I'm much longer.'

'I see.'

'I may hang around long enough to see you and Curran safely hitched, then I'll fly back.'

Nicola looked at him with startled eyes. 'I – I don't know that Curran and I are going to – to get married,' she told him.

'You're a very handsome couple,' he informed her blithely, his brush busy with the grey colour of her eyes. 'And so suitable.'

'I'm not sure that we *are* suitable.' She resented his assumption that she would marry Curran, even more than she resented Curran's.

'Oh, I think you are,' he told her, blithely unaware of her frown. 'You're both good-looking, especially in your case, and you're both more or less the same age, though I'd guess you were quite a bit younger than Curran.'

'I'm twenty-one,' she stated firmly, and he smiled.

'A baby!'

'I'm *not* a baby, Mitch, and if you go on saying it I'll – I'll—'

He chuckled deeply and looked up at her. 'You'll what?' he taunted.

'I'll walk out of here and you can finish your blessed portrait from memory!'

'You would too,' he said, but seemed unconcerned about it.

'Mitch!'

'I think I've got that blaze of glory in your eyes nicely now,' he told her, and Nicola clenched her hands on her lap and glared at him.

'I just never learn, do I?' she said ruefully. 'You always make me do what you want for your blessed painting and then look all – all smug and pleased with yourself. Well, it isn't clever, it's sheer cunning.'

He tapped the side of his nose with one painty finger and grinned at her. 'It's a cunning that comes with age,' he informed her. 'That's what I mean. If you'd lived as long as I have, you'd see through me and I'd never get the expression I want from you.'

'Oh – Methuselah!'

'That's right,' he agreed amiably. 'Now sit still just a little longer, honey, and I'll have your eyes finished.'

'Wait until you get to my mouth and I'll stick my tongue out,' she threatened.

'Tch! What manners!'

She subsided, unwillingly, but unable to find a suitable retort, and looked out of the window. 'The mist's clearing,' she said after a while, and he looked up.

'Are you riding this afternoon?'

She turned, a small frown of doubt between her

brows as she was reminded of yesterday's eventful journey. 'I – I don't know,' she said. 'Not unless Curran can come with me, I expect.'

'I see.'

She laughed shortly. 'I wish *I* did,' she confessed. 'I don't know quite what to do for the best sometimes. I'd love to go riding again, but Curran made such a fuss about me going yesterday that I'm not sure I should go without him.'

'And I've no desire to upset the course of young love,' he told her solemnly. 'So you'd better not be seen with me again.'

She stuck out her chin at that, and a gleam came into her eyes that darkened them to a stormy grey. 'If I *want* to be seen with you, or anyone else,' she declared firmly, 'I shall. I won't be dictated to by anybody.'

'I rather thought that's what you were prepared to do,' he said softly, without looking up. 'You said you wouldn't ride again without him.'

She bit her lip, frowning doubtfully. 'I wish – Mitch, what do you think I should do?'

He stopped work for a moment and looked at her steadily, then he laughed and raised his hands. 'Don't ask me, honey, I'm nobody's Dutch uncle.'

'You're not very helpful.'

'No, I guess I'm not; playing the father figure to love's young dream isn't my style at all.'

'I – I wasn't asking you to be a father figure.'

'Good.'

'Oh, Mitch, don't be so difficult! You know more

about – about these things than I do. And Curran is your cousin, you should know him better than I do.'

'You're his fiancée,' he replied, '*you* should know him better than I do.'

'I don't. And I'm not his fiancée. I've already been through all that with Curran. I haven't promised to marry him, and that's what would make me his fiancée.'

'You mean you're keeping him in suspense?' She bit her lip and did not answer and he shook his head slowly. 'You hard-hearted little devil, he's crazy about you, don't you know that?'

'He was crazy about Fiona,' she retorted impulsively, 'once upon a time!'

'So-o-o, that's it.' He stopped work and looked across at her steadily. 'I don't think it's quite the same thing, honey.'

'I wish I knew,' Nicola said despairingly. 'I just don't know what to do about Curran. He wants to marry me and I sometimes think I love him enough to marry him, but then—' She glanced up and her eyes were dark and shadowed. 'I think I should pack up and go back home,' she said slowly. 'It might be best in the long run.'

'Who for?'

She looked puzzled. 'Why – I don't know, everyone concerned, I suppose. Curran could think about it again and I could stand back and try to sort out how I *really* feel.'

'It might be a good idea,' he agreed, and she looked

at him uncertainly for a moment.

'You – you think so?'

He nodded. 'Since you ask me, yes. I think if you stay on here Curran's going to talk you round with that little boy lost look of his and you're just crazy enough to marry him out of sheer pity.'

'You don't give me credit for much intelligence.'

He smiled slowly and cocked a brow at her. 'You're pretty bright as gals go,' he told her, 'but you're too soft-hearted, Nicky, and I'd hate to see you make a mistake.'

'I see.'

She got up from the window seat and walked across to stand beside him, looking at her own face reflected in the painted image he was working on. He had given her a sort of gamin look with a provocative kind of innocence in the eyes and she felt the colour flood into her cheeks as she looked at it.

'Is that me?'

He sat back on the high stool, looking at the painting, his head back, eyes half closed as he studied it. 'It's as I see you, sweetheart, but I might have a prejudiced view.' He turned and looked at her and, seated on the stool, he was still inches higher than she was, so that she looked determinedly at the pulse throbbing at the base of his throat. 'I think it might be as well for all concerned if you went home,' he said softly.

'Mitch!'

'Well, you asked me,' he declared, and laughed at her, taking one of her hands in his own. 'You do whatever you want to do, honey, which you will anyway, but just don't go until I've finished your picture.'

'Oh, I'd hate to inconvenience you!' she retorted.

He pulled her towards him and kissed her lightly on her mouth. 'I knew you'd see it my way,' he told her, and turned sharply when the door behind them opened. 'Hi, cousin!'

'You—' Curran's face twisted with anger, and he glared at Mitchell as if he would hit him, his fists clenched tight, his eyes blazing. 'Let go her hands!'

Nicola hastily withdrew her hands from his, and Curran looked at her for the first time. 'I guessed you were in here,' he said. 'I should have known he'd be making the most of his chances on the pretext of painting your portrait.'

'Curran, you're wrong!'

'I'm not blind, Nicola!' His anger was for her as well now, and Nicola felt her heart sink at the prospect of yet another argument about Mitchell.

'So I was holding her hands,' Mitchell told him quietly. 'That's not much to make a fuss about, is it?'

'You were kissing her again,' Curran accused, and Mitchell laughed shortly.

'If you call that kissing, pal, I don't. Now for Pete's sake stop making a mountain out of a molehill and say what you really came for.'

Curran swallowed hard, looking at Nicola again, his eyes uncertain. 'I came to see if you wanted to come riding,' he said, 'but I imagine you have other things in mind.'

'I'd like to come riding.' She saw Mitchell's brows rise and knew he was smiling ironically, but she felt horribly guilty about Curran and knew she had to go with him.

'You would?'

She nodded. 'If Mitch doesn't mind.' She turned and looked at him, her eyes appealingly big. 'I'll come and sit again tomorrow, Mitch, perhaps this afternoon if that suits you.'

He shrugged, smiling at her in a way that made her feel uneasy. 'Come any time you like, honey, I'm always free.'

She looked at Curran. 'Shall we go?' she asked, and he took her hand as they walked out of the studio. He did not notice the last, wide-eyed look that Nicola gave his cousin over her shoulder as she went, nor the raised brow that acknowledged the plea for understanding.

CHAPTER NINE

'It's almost finished,' Nicola told Curran a few days later, when he asked how the portrait was progressing. Not because he had any great interest in the picture, she felt sure, but because once it was finished she would no longer be required to sit for Mitchell. He had seemed less suspicious the past couple of days, ever since she had left Mitchell to go riding with him, and she wondered if she should make plans for leaving after all, despite Mitchell's advice.

'Thank goodness,' Curran said feelingly. 'That means you won't have to spend so much time in that blessed studio with him.'

'Oh, now don't start on that hobbyhorse again,' she pleaded. 'I don't mind sitting for Mitch, in fact it's been quite fun, and not in the way you mean either,' she added hastily. 'He's fun to be with and he makes me laugh.'

It was something she had not fully realized until now, but she actually did enjoy her sessions in the studio, despite her fairly frequent verbal battles with Mitch. They were never as serious or as intense as the ones she had with Curran, and she very often finished by laughing at herself.

'I thought you didn't like him.'

'I used not to,' she agreed. 'But he can be quite good

fun, Curran, and even though he makes me angry sometimes, he makes me laugh too.'

'It sounds very cosy,' he grudged.

'Not cosy,' she argued quietly. 'I wish you wouldn't be so suspicious of me, Curran.'

'I'm not suspicious of *you*.'

Nicola sighed deeply. 'Please!'

He hugged her to him tightly. 'Oh, darling, why don't you say you'll marry me? You'd put me out of my misery then.'

She stirred uneasily, remembering Mitchell's words on the subject, and how he had called her hard-hearted. 'I'm sorry you're miserable,' she told him. 'I didn't intend you should be, but you know I won't marry you until I'm quite sure how I feel about you, Curran, and I'm not sure I feel any different than I've ever done.' She thought of her plan to go home, seeing it as the only solution if he persisted in his proposals. 'I – I had thought of going home,' she told him, and he stopped her in her tracks and turned her round to face him. She remembered that Mitchell had told her she was just soft-hearted enough to marry him out of pity, and she steeled herself against the hurt, bewildered look in his eyes.

'Going home?' he said. 'But why? You like it here, don't you?'

'I do,' she agreed. 'But if I don't marry you, Curran, I shouldn't stay on, it's what I'm here for after all, you said so yourself, and I should leave.'

'I don't see it like that! Oh, Nicola, what's happened

to us?' He held on to her arms tightly, his eyes seeking the answer in her face. 'We used to be so right together and now – oh, I don't know! Everything seems to have gone wrong!'

'I think perhaps I shouldn't have come here,' she suggested. 'There's no place for me here, I don't belong.'

'Of course you belong,' he argued. 'You said yourself that you like the old place, and you love the country, so how can you say you don't belong?'

'I don't feel right here somehow. Your aunt doesn't like me being here, she goes out of her way to let me know how she feels about me being here.'

'I – I know and I'm sorry, darling, but – oh, what can I say. You belong here as much as anyone does and I won't let you leave just because you've got some silly idea that you don't.'

'I don't, Curran,' she insisted quietly. 'Perhaps because Fiona *does*, even now. I'm stepping into Fiona's shoes at every step, and they aren't very comfortable.'

'Oh, why does it always have to be Fiona?' he cried. 'Why does she always have to be in the way?' He held her tight, his voice muffled in her hair. 'I wish to God I'd never heard of her! It's you I want, I've wanted you from the first moment I saw you. Fiona knew that, I told her so, she knew I wanted you as I never wanted her.'

'Curran!'

She held off from him and stared at the good-looking, angry face above her. 'You told her that?'

'I told her I loved you.'

'That wasn't what you said.'

'I – I don't know what I said.' He refused to let her go and forced her to stay facing him when she would have turned and walked away from him. 'Marry me, Nicola, and we'll go away from here. Anywhere you like, I don't care, as long as you're with me.'

'But you can't,' she protested. 'Your father relies on you for the business. You can't just walk out on him like that.'

'I would for you.'

'Well, I don't want you to for me.'

'Will you stay?'

She pushed him away, needing all her strength to free herself. 'I – I don't know, Curran. I should go, I think I should, and Mitch agrees with me too.'

'Mitchell? What the devil has he got to do with it?'

She turned again and faced him, sighing. 'I spoke to him about it,' she confessed. 'I had to talk to someone,' she said. 'Someone who'd understand and not be biased either way.'

'Huh! You think *he's* unbiased?'

'Of course he is.' She knew she sounded uncertain and she saw his lip curl as he recognized it.

'You know damned well he *isn't*!' he insisted.

'I know I can talk to him without his getting angry or – or spiteful,' she declared. 'I can't talk to you like that, Curran, I just can't! You always twist everything

I say and make it sound different. I feel guilty even when I haven't done anything.'

His face had that set, cold look she was beginning to recognize and her heart sank dismally. 'I don't know what to say to that,' he told her stiffly. 'Except that I thought you understood me better than you evidently do.'

'I'm sorry.' She almost giggled wildly as she uttered the phrase that Mitch was always teasing her about.

'You've made up your mind to go home?'

'Not – not for sure I haven't,' she admitted, 'but I think it would be best, Curran.'

'You won't even stay if I ask you to?'

'Oh, Curran, please don't make it any harder for me. I don't want to hurt you and I wish you could understand—'

'Like Mitchell Grant does, no doubt!'

'Please, Curran!'

He simply stood and stared at her for a moment, then his face crumpled like a child's, and she thought for one awful moment that he would cry, instead he buried his face in her hair and held her so tightly she could not move. 'Nicola! Nicola, don't go, give me another chance, please don't go!'

Her hesitation was only brief then she put her hands to his bent head and rubbed her fingers soothingly over his hair as she would have done to a child. 'I'll stay a while longer,' she promised, husky-voiced. 'Just a little while.'

It was not going to be easy, Nicola realized, staying on at Malinbrae with Curran so anxious and his aunt so determinedly unfriendly. If Ian McCrae noticed that there was an atmosphere of unease, he gave no sign of it, but went his normal, breezy way as if everything was to his liking.

It was when she was alone with Miss McCrae after breakfast one morning that the older woman looked across at her and spoke. For her to make the first move in any conversation between them was unusual enough for Nicola to look surprised and she wondered what prompted the break from habit.

'You have decided not to go back home, Nicola?' she said.

Nicola nodded hesitantly. Evidently Curran confided in his aunt more than she had realized, unless the information had been passed on to her via her brother. 'I – I shall have to go soon, of course,' Nicola said. 'But I have promised Curran that I'll stay a little while longer.'

'He wants to marry you.' It was a statement, not question, and Nicola looked at her uneasily.

'Yes, yes, he does.'

'You have not said you will?'

Nicola shook her head, her heart doing a rapid and uneasy tattoo against her ribs. 'I haven't said I will, Miss McCrae, although he's very persuasive.'

The sharp brown eyes looked at her directly, a glint of some deep hidden emotion leading them an even harder look than usual, so that Nicola shivered involuntarily. 'Curran can be very persuasive,' she agreed in her quiet voice, 'but he can also change his mind very easily too. I hope you remember that, Nicola.'

'Miss McCrae—' She hesitated, unsure just what she could say that would enable her to get a little closer to this, cold unfriendly woman. 'I know you don't like me, I know you don't like the idea of me marrying Curran, but – well, it *is* our affair whether we marry or not.'

The thin mouth was tight and drawn and Miss McCrae raised her chin in a gesture of arrogance. 'Anyone who marries into the McCrae family,' she told her, 'is important to all of us. We are a very old and a very proud family, the wife that a son chooses is very important to us, and particularly, as in Curran's case, when he is an only son.'

'But surely any man is entitled to choose his own wife?' Nicola said, her eyes wide with disbelief. 'In this day and age how can it be anything else but a free choice? I can't see, either, Miss McCrae, that Curran should displease you so much by choosing me, I'm not someone to be ashamed of.'

'You took the place of the girl Curran *should* have married,' she was told in a voice that trembled harshly. 'Fiona was the girl for Curran and it had always been so. Had it not been for his ridiculous infatuation with you, they would have been married by now.'

Nicola bit her lip, her heart in her mouth as she faced the inevitability of Fiona, yet again. 'Fiona's death was an accident,' she insisted, trying to control her voice when it trembled and whispered. 'It was an accident, Miss McCrae, and no one can say otherwise, with any foundation.'

For a moment she thought the older woman would strike her, but she closed her eyes briefly after a second or two and self-control kept her in command of the situation. 'I *know* otherwise,' she said, her voice hard and flat. 'So does Alec – Fiona's father. *We* know what Curran did to her so that he could have you.'

'I – I know he wrote her a letter to tell her about me,' Nicola said, a hand to her throat as she felt the sudden flick of coldness in her breast.

'Do you?' The hard brown eyes held hers steadily. 'Do you know what he wrote to her, Nicola Scott? Do you know how he discarded the girl he had been going to marry?'

'He – he told me what he wrote,' Nicola whispered. 'At least he told me some of it.' She could not forget that emotional burst of confidence of Curran's when he had been imploring her to stay on at Malinbrae. '. . . she knew I wanted you as I never wanted her.'

The thin hands fumbled for a moment in the pocket of the dress she wore, then she brought out a crumpled, folded piece of paper and handed it to Nicola. 'That is Curran's last letter to Fiona,' she said quietly, and Nicola noticed that her hands were trembling. 'Read it.'

'Oh no! I couldn't!'

She shrank back from the letter as if it was a living

thing that repelled her, but Margaret McCrae was insistent and the letter was pushed into her nervous fingers. 'Read it, Nicola!'

'No, no!'

'I want you to know what kind of a man my nephew is, what kind of a man you are considering marrying.'

Nicola's eyes were wide with disbelief, and she stared at the older woman for several seconds without moving or speaking, the truth dawning on her at last. That hate that gnawed at Margaret McCrae like a canker was directed as much at her nephew as it was at Nicola. Perhaps even more so, for there was a glow of sheer malice in her eyes when she spoke of Curran. Even her family loyalty and the importance of the only son choosing the right bride had been subjugated to her bitterness in losing her one chance of happiness with Alec McNee. She wanted to punish Curran so much that she would sacrifice anything to see him lose Nicola as Fiona had lost him.

She sat for some time with the crumpled letter in her hands, her eyes bright with tears of confusion. If only she could turn to someone, if Curran was here to lend her support even. Then, almost without realizing it, she unfolded the letter and tried to focus her gaze on the words, scrawled across the page in Curran's familiar, untidy handwriting.

'*Fiona,*' no endearment preceded her name. '*I wish you had not written the way you did, you make things very difficult for me. I'm sorry if you think I've treated*

173

you badly, but there's nothing I can do about the way I feel about my darling Nicola. I love her as I never loved you, or ever could, and I cannot give her up no matter what you threaten. I don't believe you would do anything foolish and I won't be blackmailed like that. If you think it will make me change my mind, you should know me better. Don't be tempted into making a gesture, Fiona, you'll be the only loser. I just don't love you any more and there's nothing I can do about it.' There followed the big scrawled, '*Curran*' that she had seen so often at the bottom of her own letters.

Her fingers clenched tightly on the worn paper and she felt the tears rolling down her cheeks as she sat huddled in the armchair. Margaret McCrae said nothing, but she gently prised her fingers apart and took the crumpled letter from her.

'I – I didn't believe it,' Nicola whispered at last. 'I just didn't believe it.'

The other woman still did not speak, but there was an expression on her sharp face that betrayed perhaps a hint of remorse, and she shook her head slowly. 'I wanted you to know,' was all she said, and Nicola could stand no more.

There was a tension in the big sunny room that was almost unbearable and that cold, stern woman sitting there so righteous and unthinkingly malicious made her long to escape. She got to her feet, one hand brushing away the tears that blinded her, and went to the door, going out into the hall without turning.

Nor did she hesitate in the direction she took, but

went straight to the low door beside the stairs, and through into the east wing.

Mitchell was already there this morning and for a moment she paused in the doorway of the studio, her hands clenched tightly. He turned and saw her then, and the smile that had been ready to greet her vanished in a second as he moved swiftly across the long room towards her.

'Nicky!'

Strong arms enfolded her and she did not hesitate to lay her face against the softness of his shirt, her arms tight around him as she cried in real earnest. She did not care that she looked dishevelled or that the hands that held her were covered in paint, it was just so good to be held so reassuringly that she did not care about anything else.

'Nicky?'

He lifted her chin at last and looked down at her tear-stained face with a very slight smile crooking his mouth at its corners. One hand smoothed back the thick tawny-coloured hair from her forehead and he kissed her, very gently, just beside her left ear.

'I'm – I'm sorry, Mitch.'

'That old tale again?' He was teasing her, but gently, and she shook her head slowly.

'I really am,' she assured him. 'I had no right to make such an exhibition of myself and drag you into my problems.'

'You've got problems?' He was still brushing back the thick hair from her brow and the movement was almost hypnotic so that she half closed her eyes.

'I – I've been talking to Miss McCrae.'

He flicked a brow upwards, his expression curious. 'Aunt Margaret? That must have been an event in itself. She isn't given to talking to you, is she?'

'No.' She rubbed at her eyes to dismiss the remaining tears and he reached into his pocket and handed her a big white handkerchief.

'You'll have a mucky face if you rub it with *those* hands.'

She looked down at her hands and shook her head. 'It – it was the letter,' she explained. 'The ink was very dark and it came off on my hands.'

He drew her across the room and sat them both on the long seat in the window, taking her hands in his and holding them tightly. 'Suppose you start at the beginning and tell me all about it?' he suggested. 'Will that help?'

She nodded. 'It will,' she said. 'At least I think it will, there's not much anyone can do now. I shall have to leave here and—'

'Whoa!' He shook her lightly. 'Start at the beginning, you're running on like a little whirlwind, slow down and wait for me.'

She smiled in spite of the way she felt and thought how lucky it was that she had instinctively come through into the east wing to Mitchell. Curran would never have been so comfortingly calm.

'You – you remember what Mrs. McKie told us about Fiona?' she began, and he looked at her narrowly.

'Fiona again. Hasn't that ghost been laid yet?'

Nicola shook her head. 'She never will be at Malinbrae,' she told him huskily. 'She *did* crash her car deliberately, Mitch.'

He said nothing for a while, only sat there holding her hands in that gentle, reassuring way with his blue eyes half hidden by their unusually long lashes. 'How do you know?' he asked then.

'Because I've seen a – a letter.'

'Oh?' He looked at her, expecting her to continue, and she looked down at their clasped hands, seeking the right words. It was not as easy as she had expected.

'Miss McCrae has a letter,' she said. 'The last letter that Curran wrote to – to Fiona.'

'And she showed it to you?'

'Yes.'

His frown was a straight dark line across his brow and she saw his mouth set tightly until he looked as formidable as Margaret McCrae. 'They spare you nothing, this family, do they?' he said. 'Why did she do it, Nicky?'

'Because – because she wanted me to know—' He looked at her steadily. 'She wanted me to know what kind of a man Curran was.'

'I see.'

'You're not surprised?'

He shook his head. 'No. I guessed all along it was Curran she was directing her venom at, and not you.

177

You only got the backlash, poor little darling.'

She glanced up at him sharply, but decided not to say anything at the moment. Perhaps the endearment had slipped out without his noticing it. 'I hadn't realized how much she disliked him, Mitch. It – it made my blood run cold the way she hates him. And all because he prevented her marriage to Alec McNee.'

'I'm wondering if he did,' Mitchell mused, sidetracking for a moment. 'If Alec McNee really wanted to marry her, he would have been more likely to turn to her in his grief than turn away from her, surely, even if Curran is her nephew.'

'Hmm.' Nicola considered it for a moment. 'It is a bit odd when I think of it.'

'No doubt she believed it was because of Curran that she didn't get the expected proposal, though, and that's why she started trying to split up you and him.'

She shook her head, feeling the tears in her eyes again as she looked out of the window. 'Oh, Mitch, why did I ever come here? Why didn't I stay at home and – and go on as I was?'

He smiled at that, and one finger raised her chin, tracing the despondent lines beside her mouth. 'I guess there was some mysterious reason fate had in mind,' he told her softly. 'Cheer up, little one, it isn't the end of the world yet.'

'It's the end of anything between Curran and me,' Nicola said with an air of finality, and he lifted her chin again to look at her.

'You're going home?'

'I have to now,' she said. 'I read that letter, Mitch, I couldn't stay on after that. I just couldn't bear it.'

'Fiona had the last word?'

She raised her eyes, wide and vulnerable and darkly grey. 'Wasn't she bound to?' she asked.

CHAPTER TEN

NICOLA felt a coward about telling Curran she was leaving Malinbrae. She could not bring herself to let him know she had read that callous and cold-blooded letter he had written to Fiona, no matter how much she thought about it. It would be enough to say that she had finally made up her mind to go, and leave it at that.

He was not yet back from some estate business which had taken him most of the day, and she faced the prospect of dinner with little pleasure. Ian McCrae had taken the news of her impending departure with a curious blend of regret and relief, so that she wondered how much he had been told by his sister.

He was perfectly polite and said he had enjoyed having her there, but she had the feeling, as she often had before, that he found her presence a little embarrassing. Probably because of his sister's attitude towards her.

It was a mellow, sunny afternoon, and Nicola sighed as she paused in her packing to look out of the window. The garden already had a sadder air about it as chrysanthemums came into bud to replace the earlier, summer flowers, and there was a hazy, dreamlike mist round the distant hills that gave them an unreal look that was quite beautiful. There was much she would miss at Malinbrae, despite the moments of anxiety and upset she had known there.

She thought of Mitchell down there in the east wing, and the portrait he would now have to complete from memory. It was finished to all intents, but there were touches to add that would make perfection of an already excellent work.

Mitch had been amused by her admiration of it, and teased her that it was a form of conceit to admire her own likeness so much, but there was something about the portrait that enchanted her and she never tired of looking at it. Of trying to discover which of her various moods he had captured her in.

Pulling herself up sharply, she saw Curran coming from the stable yard beyond the garden, and felt her heart start to race wildly when she thought of the task that faced her. He looked so comfortingly familiar from up here at her window, as she had seen him so many times before, that it was still difficult for her to believe that he could have written that heartless letter to Fiona McNee.

He wore riding clothes, and above the collar of the white shirt his face looked fresh and boyish, and very good-looking. His stride covered the garden path in a very short time and, as he neared the house, he glanced up and saw her, raising one hand in greeting, a smile lighting his eyes.

Nicola returned the greeting, biting on her lower lip as she turned away from the window when he was out of sight. It would not be easy telling him she was going and she would much rather have remembered him as he was now, than cold and angry or childishly petulant and anxious, as he would surely be when he had heard what she had to say.

She packed most of her things and left one suitcase open to take the rest in the morning. After dinner she would have to ring and arrange for Malin's one and only taxi to come and fetch her in time for the ten o'clock train tomorrow. It was all very clear and concise in her mind now; there would be no turning back, no matter how Curran pleaded.

She had given herself little time to wait before dinner and the family were just going in as she arrived downstairs. 'Darling!' Curran came across to her and pulled her to him, but she avoided too close an embrace and turned her head away when he tried to kiss her. 'Nicola?'

They followed Ian and Margaret McCrae into the big dining-room and Nicola knew Curran was not only curious but anxious, but she fought the temptation to be drawn into discussing her leaving until after the meal was over and they were alone.

He watched her closely and anxiously all through dinner, and conversation was only spasmodic, Ian McCrae making most of the effort. Miss McCrae looked at her once or twice as if she was curious to know what exactly she was going to do, but she said nothing and Nicola volunteered nothing. The older woman, she thought, seemed less tense than she had ever seen her and she wondered if she would let her nephew know that she had been ultimately responsible for Nicola leaving.

As soon as it was possible Curran got up from the table and came round to Nicola, catching her arm and making sure she did not elude him. His good-looking face was determinedly cheerful as he led her out into the garden, and he looked down at her curiously when she managed to evade his encircling arm.

'Is something wrong, darling?' he asked, and Nicola shook her head.

'I'm leaving, Curran, that's all. I wanted to tell you when we were alone so that you wouldn't be embarrassed.'

'Embarrassed?' He stopped her short and tried to turn her face to him, but she resisted him and walked on so that he was obliged to follow if he wanted to talk to her. 'I'm hurt, Nicola, not embarrassed,' he told her. 'Why? Why are you going when you promised to stay on? Why?'

'Because I think it's best, Curran.' She tried to control her voice, but it shook terribly and sounded husky and breathless. 'Please don't make a scene,' she begged, before he could speak. 'It's best that I go; I want to go, and your – your family understand.'

'Well, I don't!' She did not look at him, but she knew he had that tight, set look on his face again, and she regretted it more than she could say. 'I don't *want* you to go, you know how I feel. How can you be so – so callous and unfeeling?'

'So—' She spun round and stared at him, the betraying words trembling on her lips, but she bit them back in time and turned back to continue walking. 'Please don't make a scene, Curran. I've already packed most of my things and I have to ring the taxi man and ask him to come and fetch me in time for the ten o'clock train tomorrow morning. There's really no more to be said, except that I'm sorry.'

'Tomorrow?' He gripped her arm and brought her to a halt, his fingers digging into her flesh as he brought her round to face him. '*Now* I understand. I might have known it.'

'I – I don't understand, Curran.'

'No?' His brown eyes were stone hard as he looked down at her. 'It wouldn't have anything to do with the fact that Mitchell leaves in the morning too, would it?'

'Mitch?' She stared at him wide-eyed, her heart racing wildly. 'Mitch leaves tomorrow?'

'As if you didn't know!'

'I didn't, Curran.' She remembered how she had cried on his shoulder that morning, how they had talked, and never once had he betrayed the fact that he was leaving Malinbrae. It hurt that he had not confided in her, more than she cared to admit.

'He decided to move out a couple of days ago,' he jeered. 'Don't tell me you didn't know. Oh, for heaven's sake, Nicola, don't treat me like a complete fool!'

'Curran, I swear I didn't know.'

'And I don't believe you!' His expression banished

any suggestion of good looks as he looked down at her with those hard eyes that were so much like his aunt's. 'Making out you were sitting for your portrait!' he went on harshly. 'Not that I've ever really believed you. You've been having an affair with him, right under my nose, and I'll bet you found it very funny, the pair of you. Don't bother to deny it,' he added sharply, when she would have spoken, and Nicola curled her hands into tight little fists, pulling her arm free of his grip.

If he was so sure, so certain she had been behaving as badly towards him as he had to Fiona, then he really deserved to be hurt. 'All right,' she informed him huskily, her cheeks burning bright and her chin defiantly angled. 'I've been having an affair with Mitch – *now* are you satisfied?'

He stood there for a moment, his face cold and unrelenting in the evening light and she felt her heart sink when he turned on his heel and walked back into the house without another word. It was not how she had wanted it to end at all.

Nicola awoke early next morning and lay for a while watching the first haze of gold sunlight pierce the September mist, changing the sky beyond her window. She would not go down to breakfast, she had already decided, then she would not have to see Curran again, for he would not have changed his attitude overnight, she knew him well enough to know that. He had been nowhere in sight the previous evening when she returned to the house, and she had not seen him since.

Her taxi was due to come for her just after nine. She had given him plenty of time to negotiate that dreadful road, so she left it as late as she could before she went downstairs. Miss McCrae had bade her a brief goodbye the night before, and Ian McCrae shook her hand heartily and wished her well when she came downstairs.

Mrs. Johnston, she thought, was almost sorry to see her go, and Nicola wished that others could have been so malleable. She thanked the housekeeper for taking care of her when she was injured, and shook her hand. 'It's a pity it couldnae have been different,' the woman said softly. 'Goodbye, Miss Scott.'

The house seemed silent and somehow sad as Nicola looked around the big hall that had so impressed her on her arrival, and remembering that day she smiled when she thought of Mitch's part in the arrival. She still felt hurt and puzzled that Mitch had not told her he was leaving, especially when he had known for several days, apparently.

She must go and see him, if he was not already gone, and the thought that he might be sent her hurrying to the little door into the east wing. She ran the length of the corridor, suddenly anxious in case he should not be there, and she flung open the door of the studio, breathing erratically and holding her throat, her eyes anxious.

'Mitch!'

He turned from the window as she came in and for a

moment she felt sure he frowned, then the familiar slow smile crooked his mouth and her pulse responded as it always did.

'Is your taxi here?' he asked, and she shook her head, the blood pounding at her temple until she could hear it like a drumbeat.

'No, it isn't quite time yet.'

The studio was empty of all those canvases round the walls and had a bare, neglected look, with the high stool he used to perch on, set alone in the middle of the floor. Only one canvas remained in view and from the size and shape of it, she recognized her own portrait.

'I – I thought you'd be gone,' she said.

'Not yet.'

She walked across to the window and, as she approached, he left his place by the window seat and went over to perch on the stool, hooking one heel in the crossbar as he always did. 'You didn't tell me you were leaving,' she accused, trying to make him meet her eyes. It was not like him to avoid her gaze and she held her hands tightly together as she looked at him. 'Why, Mitch?'

'Why am I going?'

'No. Why didn't you tell me?' She realized suddenly that she had no real right to expect him to tell her his plans and she shook her head hastily. 'No, I shouldn't have asked you that,' she said. 'I haven't any right to ask questions.'

'That's right,' he agreed quietly, a crook of a smile on his mouth. 'Little girls should be seen and not heard.'

'I'll ignore that, as it's – it's the last time I shall see you.' She bit her lip then, realization dawning that it could well be the last time she would ever see him.

'I intended sneaking out before you were up this morning,' he told her, and she frowned.

'Why? Why would you do that?'

He looked up then and smiled, ruefully. 'It was my safety device,' he told her. 'You know how I hate the idea of the noose being thrown around my neck, honey.'

'Oh, Mitch!' She looked across the room at him perched there on the high stool as she had so often seen him.

'Do I gather that Cousin Curran has escaped the noose?' he asked softly, and she nodded, remembering suddenly her last words to Curran last night.

'I – I told him—' She looked at him from under her lashes, judging his reaction. 'I told him I'd been having an affair with you,' she said.

'You did what?' He kicked at the footbar for a moment. 'Do you mind telling me why?' She thought he was taking it quite well, but since he would not meet her eyes she could not be absolutely sure.

'It was his fault,' she said defensively. 'He *said* I'd been – I'd been having an affair with you all the time you'd been painting my portrait, and – I lost my temper and agreed with him.'

'Result?'

She glanced at him through her lashes. 'He believed me,' she said, 'and walked off in a furious temper. It's all over.'

'What about our affair?' he asked softly. 'Is that supposed to be all over too?'

'Oh, Mitch, I—'

Her small oval face looked all eyes, huge and darkly grey below that thick tawny hair, and her lips were parted slightly as she sought to explain her own impulsive action.

'You're such a baby,' he said softly, and she shook her head.

'Would you really have gone away without saying goodbye to me?' she asked.

He shrugged. 'Even old campaigners like me get carried away sometimes,' he admitted lightly. 'I guess that's why I'm still here. I wanted to see you again though heaven knows you're very bad for my blood pressure and I hate to think what my temperature's doing at the moment.'

She walked across the studio and stood beside him, one finger tracing the line of his sleeve. Her pulse was banging away at her temple and her legs felt so weak she wondered how she was still managing to stand. 'I – I won't be able to help you finish my picture,' she said, and he laughed softly, glancing at the covered canvas on the window seat.

'I've finished it,' he told her. 'I had thought of leaving it for Curran, but maybe I'd better not after all.'

'You – you don't want it?'

A hand reached out and gently touched her cheek. 'It's a poor substitute for the real thing,' he said quietly.

'Mitch!'

The long legs unhooked themselves from the stool and he stood up. There was a kind of tense restraint about him that communicated itself to her, and she felt her hands trembling as she held them tightly together. Then his hands circled her waist and he pulled her towards him, a pressure she did not attempt to resist, and he looked down at her for a long, breathless minute in silence.

'I hadn't meant this to happen,' he told her, his voice deep and soft. 'That's why I was going before I saw you again.'

'I'd have cried my heart out if you'd gone without seeing me,' she told him softly. 'Then you'd have been sorry, wouldn't you?'

'Maybe.' His dark face with its blue eyes shadowed and intense, so close she could see the tiny lines etched round his mouth, filled her vision for a moment, then he drew her closer until she was held breathlessly tight in his arms. His mouth found hers, gently at first, then more fiercely, almost hungrily, until she felt her head spinning with the throbbing of the pulse in her temple.

He kissed her neck and the smooth creaminess of her throat, his face buried in her tawny hair, while she hugged tight to the lean hardness of him as if she would never let him go. He rested his chin on the top of her head at last, and his laugh reverberated through her body. 'I hope you know what you're letting yourself in for, sweetheart,' he said.

Nicola lifted her face to him, and he kissed the tip of her nose. 'What am I letting myself in for?' she asked.

'A guy who's ill-bred, uncouth, lacking in polish—'

'Oh, Mitch!' She tiptoed and stemmed the words with her mouth. 'I love you.'

He sighed deeply. 'And I love you, God help me,' he said. 'I never thought I'd ever take kindly to the noose I've beeen avoiding for so long. Especially when it's slipped round my unsuspecting neck by a beautiful little half-pint hardly out of her cradle. It's not fair the way you snuck up on me, honey.'

'I don't like being called honey,' she teased, her eyes glistening with laughter, and he kissed her again long and hard.

'Then you'll just have to get used to it,' he told her. 'And that, unless I'm very much mistaken, is your taxi arrived.'

'Oh!' She looked at him wide-eyed, dismayed at the idea of having to leave him.

'I'll go and send him away,' he told her.

'But, Mitch, I – I can't stay here.'

'Neither can I,' he told her cheerfully. 'I'm taking you home,' he added in a voice that brooked no argument. 'All the way. I want to have a word with your folks and let them know that my intentions are honourable.' He cocked a quizzical brow at her as he reached the door. 'I hope they've got no racial prejudice,' he said, and Nicola shook her head, her eyes shining softly.

'They've got nothing against Americans,' she told him. 'It's only me.'

He swept that swift disturbing glance over her from head to foot. 'When I get back,' he promised darkly as he left the room, 'I'll do something about that.'